BILLIONAIRE BODYGUARD

BROTHERHOOD PROTECTORS WORLD

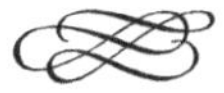

KENDRA MEI CHAILYN

BROTHERHOOD PROTECTORS
Billionaire Bodyguard
Kendra Mei Chailyn

Sometimes, being your brother's keeper is a trap…

Tianna Sharp's brother did a bad thing.

Now he's dead, leaving her holding the bag. When the danger comes to her doorstep, Tianna goes to the only man she knows can help her and the last man she knows will want to. Montana isn't happy to see her, but she doesn't really have a choice.

It was supposed to be simple enough—find out who is after Tianna and handle the problem. But the moment Maksim "Hermes" Demidov meets Tianna he knows immediately there won't be anything simple about any of this—especially where his body and heart are concerned.

But he must keep his hands to himself—she's nothing but trouble. Usually, Maksim takes it all in stride, but Tianna's type of trouble, he can do without.

To make matters worse, Tianna's brother has brought back a mistake from the Brotherhood Protectors' past and if Maksim isn't not careful, it could burn their world to the ground.

WHENEVER MY BROTHER did bad things, I suffered. Our parents were killed in an accident in Canada years before and I felt it was my responsibility to protect him from everything. Most often than not, he walked into bad situations as if he was invincible. It was almost like he looked for the worst kind of trouble to ruin his life and mine.

And each time I swore it would be the last time, I realized the only way it would be the last time was if he was dead.

And Joseph Sharp was dead.

His death had left me in a precarious position—one that threatened to kill me as well and I wasn't okay with that.

Frowning, I zipped my purse closed, strung it over my shoulder and descended the elevator of the office building I owned. I'd remained behind to field a call from an international client.

It had taken longer than it should.

The language barrier hadn't helped.

Strange—the parking lot was completely empty. Eerie wasn't the word I would use to describe it, but my mind was exhausted from the length of my day. Still, I stopped long enough to remove the mace from my purse, held it tightly in one hand and made my way across the lot to where my car was.

Usually, I parked closer to the door in my reserved spot. But there had been some needed repairs and they were yet to finish the construction.

My stilettos dragged across the asphalt in my haste. My heart slammed inside me as if it was trying to escape.

Fishing my keys from the side of my purse, I quickened my steps toward the vehicle. I hit the remote to kill the alarm and unlock the driver's side. The lights to the sports car flashed, the vehicle chirped and—

BOOM!

The force of the explosion sent me flying across the parking lot. The heat of it searing my skin and blinding me to the world around. Somewhere during my flight, the keys and mace slipped from my fingers and was lying somewhere in the lot.

My focus was on not letting my skull connect with the ground. I dropped my chin while trying to twist my body to hit on the meaty part of my side. But I failed and made it worse—landing half on my side, half on my back.

I didn't need a doctor to tell me I'd either bruise or cracked a rib or two.

The arm I'd landed on throbbed and I wiggled my fingers, thankfully I hadn't broken anything there. My face was on fire and every muscle in my body tightened as if to protect themselves. Pain raged through me, causing me to curl into a ball, as I covered my head with my arms, trying to stop the hurt of debris. Hot pieces fell around me, on me, singing into my skin, making me grit my teeth against the pain.

It wasn't everyday my car erupted into a ball of fire.

I rolled to my back, gritted my teeth and hauled myself off the ground. Glancing around, I staggered away from what was left of my car, stopping only to grab my purse. Someone was bound to see the flames and called the cops. I couldn't stay on the scene because they would have questions. I had no answers except that my brother was an idiot who pissed off someone and died before he could tell me what he'd done.

It was always one thing after another with him and this time his screwup was permanent. This time, I was left holding the bag of whatever fuckery he'd pulled this time.

By the time I managed to catch a cab home, my body was throbbing even more. The adrenaline was still pushing me to do things and I worried about how I would crash once the adrenaline wore off.

But that was future me's problem.

The cops would catch up to me sooner or later. I needed to make sure I didn't look as if my ass wasn't just lit on fire.

I rushed into the house and found some aspirins in the bathroom. Though it said to take one, I popped two with an entire glass of water, then hurried through the bedroom, gathering a few things.

I couldn't stay at my house. They'd already paid me one visit and blew up my vehicle. I doubt I'd survive another visit.

After packing a bag with a few necessities, I gathered my important papers, traveller's cheques and the Springfield XDM from where I had it taped to the wall behind my headboard. I quickly checked the chamber, ensured the safety was on and shove it into my purse.

This time, I climbed behind the wheel of my BMW sedan and sped away from my house, checking over my shoulders repeatedly to ensure I was alone. My street was quiet, a cul-de-sac that backed up to a river.

The traffic wasn't much.

I would have been able to see if someone was following.

But the silence, the lack of movement—all of it scared me.

Once I was checked into an out of the way motel, I did what I always did when I was in trouble. I reverted to Hank "Montana" Patterson—a man I was pretty sure was tired of seeing me, tired of hearing me, tired of even remembering that I existed.

I hadn't been the best person to him in the past. But he was a good man and it killed me to always be depending on him the way I had in the last three years. But Joseph was an idiot and I kept falling for his little cons which usually left me crawling back to Montana for help.

As I dialed the number I now knew by heart, I wondered if this would be the one time he said no.

"Yes?" His voice crisp, cold, hard.

"We need to talk." I managed.

"About what?"

"Joseph."

"Meet me at the same place in an hour." He hung up.

My heart broke.

I knew what I'd done to him. I knew he had the right to hate me, to leave me to whatever darkness I'd fallen into. I deserved that venom from him.

But I was a woman in danger and Montana had never been the kind of person to turn his back in that kind of situation. He was a gorgeous man with a heart of gold and a body of steel. I'd be an idiot to not have a small part of me still wanting him. That same part of me ached for a soft word from him—no matter how tiny.

Yes, I knew he had someone else. Joseph had told me that he heard from a friend Montana had long since moved on. According to Joseph, she was gorgeous, and perfect. He'd also told me this woman loved Montana in a way that was almost supernatural.

The day I heard my heart broke into a million little pieces. I spent the next few hours drinking, crying and feeling all kinds of jealous feelings for this new woman.

I knew the kind of man Montana was, the kind of lover he was, the way he took care of his woman. It wasn't a secret he wouldn't have stayed single for long. Sooner or later, a smarter woman than I had been would come along and snatched him up.

It was my fault I wasn't *that* woman. I had the chance to be and I blew it.

I pulled my mind from what could have been and refocused on the present.

There were Canadian assholes coming for me.

As quickly as I could, I checked my purse for the weapon then hurried out to meet Montana at the diner we usually met when my world turned into a giant dumpster fire. It wasn't a far drive, but I took my time, being careful not to break any traffic laws to avoid getting pulled over.

If nothing else, the cops were probably waiting for a search of my car to see if I was in it when it turned into a fourth of July fire show.

That gave me a little time to get the hell out of dodge.

I sat in the parking lot watching people go in and out of the diner. At first, I told myself I was waiting there to see if someone had followed me to the meet. Then I realized I was stalling. I was trying to suck in enough courage to tell Montana that Joseph had screwed up again and I needed his help—

Again.

How do I tell Montana that I once again stepped in to help my brother and wound up on the wrong side of some very dangerous people?

Holding my breath for a second, I checked my face in the mirror then slid my sunglasses over my eyes. Once I pushed myself out of the car and slammed the door, I looked around to ensure I wasn't being followed then jogged across the parking lot.

Inside, I ignored the hostess and fell into the booth across from Montana. For a silent second, I did nothing—hell, I didn't think I was even breathing.

I used those moments to adjust my shirt and removed my sunglasses.

If I was to be honest with myself, I would admit he was sexier than I remembered. But Hank and I had been there, done that and as good as he looked, I didn't want to go there again.

He was a good man.

I was an idiot and from the ring on his finger I knew I would be barking up the absolute wrong tree.

Swallowing the jealousy that formed a lump in my throat, I exhaled and lifted my eyes to him. His brown eyes were suspicious, hard—almost cold.

I licked my lips.

"How are you, Montana?" I asked.

"Why don't you tell me what you want?" He cut to the chase. "You only come around when you want something."

"That's not my fault. The last time I saw you." I glanced around then back at him. "The last time I saw you, you said to only call if I was bleeding to death or dead."

"Well." He folded his arms across his massive chest. "I guess I wasn't clear enough. You're not dead. And you're definitely not bleeding to death. So, I'm going to ask one final time—what do you want?"

"Why're you like this to me?"

"Because you're my past and even though I'm over you, I don't want to keep seeing you." He growled. "Because you and Joseph should come with a warning label."

The waitress appeared at our side. I ordered burger and fries and a cola. When she was finally gone again, I rubbed the back of my neck and continued. "I'm sorry about—"

"I don't want to hear it." He told me. "I think we've figured out years ago that your apologies mean nothing. So, again—what do you want?"

"Joseph is dead." I told him.

Montana said nothing. He was still crossed with me.

"You don't look surprised."

For the first time, he quirked a brow at me. "Joseph had a habit of kicking people when they're down. He likes stabbing them in the back and making off with things that doesn't belong to me. It was only a matter of time."

"You can't mean that."

"When have I ever lied to you?" Montana countered.

I swallowed the lump in my throat. "He pissed off some people in Toronto. When he called for help, I tried helping, even though I knew this could only end in my tears, he was my brother, and he was in trouble. But he said he'd call me back with more info and the next think I know, I'm on a flight into Toronto to pick up his body. Then, I barely had time to put him in the ground before the people he crossed came calling."

"What do they want?"

"I don't know."

"What did I tell you about lying to me, Tianna?" Montana leaned forward.

"I'm not lying." I promised. "I don't know what they're after. Before that recent call, I hadn't spoken to Joseph in about six months. The last time he showed up at my place here he brought some chick with him saying she was pregnant."

"Was she?"

"Was she what?" I asked.

Montana gave me a look that told me he was ready to burn my world to the ground. And it wasn't in the way I wanted him to—with his beautiful eyes and that well toned body. No, he wanted to literally throw gasoline on it and set it ablaze.

"No. She wasn't pregnant." I exhaled and offered him a sheepish smile. "They were trying to get me to *lend* him some money so he could *invest* in some company out of Indiana. I didn't give them any money. I didn't even let them in. When I received the call that I should pick up his body, I thought it was another one of his little scams. But when the coroner did a video chat with me to show me the body for identification, I realized the truth.

It was no joke."

"How did he die?"

"They said it was a suicide."

"Please." Montana leaned back in the booth, his muscular arm stretched along the edge of the seat.

"Joseph is too much of an asshole to kill himself. Tell me about the men who came after you."

"They're from Toronto." I replied. "They said Joe took something from them and I had a week to give it back. The thing is, I have no idea what *it* is. There wasn't really anything in his personal effects when they gave the little bag to me. I don't even know to look or even what to look for. After a week, someone blew up my car."

"Well, I think it's safe to say what happened to your car was a warning." Montana rubbed his eyes. "If they wanted you dead, you would be."

"That's reassuring."

He frowned at me. "They're not going to kill you until they find what they're looking for."

"That's reassuring." I grumbled again.

"I wasn't trying to be." Montana tossed back. "The help you need is in Toronto. I can't go with you. There are things I have to do right now, and Sadie would kill me if I took off to Toronto with my ex."

"Her name is Sadie…"

"Don't—even."

I nodded. "Does she know you're here—with me?"

"Before we go any further You should know one thing." His eyes screamed a warning at me. "Because of you, I know what secrets do to a relationship. I hide nothing from Sadie. But if you go after her, I will end you—got it?"

I hung my head.

In that moment, I realized I was ashamed to say, the old me would have tried something. The old me would have lied and manipulated to get them to break up. A little part of the new me thought about it for a very brief second.

If Montana was any other man, maybe I would have reverted to that horrible personality I once was. But he was good and true, and it would kill me to hurt him again.

Honestly, I hadn't been that spoiled, bitter woman for a long while.

Testing the waters, to see if there was a chance had been a kneejerk reaction.

Knowing he had someone else told me Karma had finally made its way back around to me. I couldn't outrun it forever—I knew that.

My food arrived and I nibbled away at some of the French fries as he made a few phone calls. Though I should be afraid, I couldn't help thinking about what I'd lost with Montana. All he had wanted was me. But I was too focused on myself to give him much of anything. He'd waited, been patient but while my brother was into hair-brained schemes, I tended to say things without thinking.

Before I knew it, I'd burned that bridge and Montana was raging.

"Okay." Montana's voice brought me back to my trouble. "Whatever your brother stole should still be in Toronto. I have a friend there who's agreed to help you figure things out."

"But…"

"That's the deal, Tianna." He told me. "Take it or leave it."

"And if I don't take it?" I demanded.

There I go again. Saying things without thinking.

"Then our retainer is a hundred thousand dollars. I'll assign you one of our Canadians to help you." His eyes were hard, dark—the very flames of hell burning in them. "Like I told you before, I won't disrespect my girl by being caught in another one of your little games."

"You protect her like you never protected me."

Montana laughed—a cold sound that made me want to hide. "You think I'm protecting her? Sadie doesn't require my protection. But you might."

My body took in an involuntary breath, soft. "I'll take it."

His words sucked the wind out of my sails. Hearing he'd found a wife who took care of him like I should have broke me.

Montana dropped money on the table and stood to his full, overpowering height. "Let's go."

We left the diner and made our way back into Eagle Rock. I wasn't much of a nature person but even I was transfixed by the beauty of the Crazy Mountains. But I didn't have time to really take them in. Before I knew what was happening, I was sitting in a living room, surrounded by some familiar faces—Axel "Swede" Svenson, Tate "Bear" Parker and Joseph "Kujo" Kuntz. They hadn't been happy to see me.

I couldn't say I blamed them.

"Where's Six?" I asked Kujo.

"Home." He replied tersely.

I nodded, feeling as if I'd once again said the wrong thing.

With the plan in place, the others set to work. As I rose to follow Kujo out the door, Montana stopped me.

"This is the last time, Tianna." He informed me. "Make this count."

Before I could reply, he stepped around me and through the door.

The tone in his voice told me he was serious—that he'd never been more serious about anything —ever.

I wanted to die.

MAKSIM DEMIDOV

JUST OUTSIDE OF HUSTLE, and bustle and chaos of Toronto, I listened to the silence being punctuated by the call of night creatures. I wasn't sure why I moved to the city after my stint in the military. It was never the best place for me before I did the whole military thing. I grew up in a small town of barely three hundred people. My idea of a perfect date was lying on my back in the belly of the pickup truck and stare up at the sky with beers in the cooler.

I'd spend hours, listening to the nothingness of a small-town.

The military happened and over the years the silence turned against me.

Looking back toward the city, the CN Tower rose upward, different colour lights streaking up the outside. The Rogers Center sat like a reminder of a time when Toronto was at the forefront of architectural technology.

I sat on the hood of my truck sipping from a bottle of soda and watching my private plane land. It touched down without incident and taxied along the private piece of land. Usually, I would have my pilot land at Billy Bishop where my private plane was stored then take the tunnel or the ferry to the mainland.

But with this favor I was doing for Montana, we didn't need to announce who was on board.

I didn't move until long after the plane came to a stop and the engine went off. Sliding to my feet, I dragged my fingers through my hair and made my way up to the aircraft.

The pilot offered me a mock salute before I was close enough to not be seen. The door opened and I jogged up the steps and entered the belly of the plane. I knew the woman seated in one of the leather seats —from the pictures Montana had sent me.

Without speaking, I fell into the seat across from her.

"You must be Montana's friend."

She lifted her eyes to me.

"Maksim Demidov." I told her simply. "They call me Hermes."

"Hermes?" She quirked a brow. "But your parents are Russian."

I watched her.

"Yet you have the name for a trickster god from Greek mythology."

I offered her a smile then. "How about I get you off this plane?" I asked instead of focusing on her confusion. "Tonight, you can get cleaned up and rest. We'll talk in the morning."

"I have to ask." Her voice was soft.

"What's your question."

"Montana calls and you drop your life to help him?" She asked. "What's the catch? What does he owe you?"

"A bottle of Jack."

"You work cheap."

"This may be a hard concept for you to grasp." I scoffed. "But Montana is a friend—a brother. He askes for the moon and I pull it from the sky and lay it at his feet—understood?"

"What's it with you, military types?" She tossed her arms up.

"It's a loyalty thing." He spat. "You wouldn't understand."

The look in her eyes told me if she could kill me and get away with it, she would have. But I didn't have time for her delicate sensibilities.

"Do you have a suitcase, a bag?"

She shook her head. "The guys didn't exactly give me time to go home and pack."

Without saying anything else, I rose and exited the plane. I saw now why Montana was so huffy with me on the phone. He'd told me the two of them had a past and while I knew Montana wasn't a virgin before Sadie, there had never been a woman to make Montana react the way he had.

This woman must have been a piece of work.

I stopped to speak with the pilot then descended the steps. Tianna followed me, slowly and it irritated me. Did she not know what we were doing was highly illegal?

"Your legs work better than this, Ms. Sharp." I told her.

"Don't talk to me like that."

I swerved on her. "Do you understand what we've done to get you into this country?" I stepped in close to growl at her. "What we're doing right now isn't exactly above board. So, move your ass!"

Tianna was taken aback but I didn't care. She probably wasn't accustomed to people speaking to her like that. From what I gathered she'd made a name for herself in the fashion world and the money never stopped rolling in. That mean, she was prob-ably surrounded by those who asked how high when she told them jump.

Her brother, on the other hand, hadn't kept a stable job—ever. He graduated high school and it was one scam after another. He ran to her when he'd done something bad and each time, she had his back. I supposed I couldn't blame her—he was, after all, her brother.

The sound of plane's engine roared to life behind us. I didn't look back. We were speeding toward the main road when the private jet shot off the ground and into the air. Though I said nothing to her, I could feel her eyes on me. It was a strange sensation, one I wasn't sure how to feel about.

"Are you hungry?" I asked.

She cleared her throat. "Yes."

"What are you craving?"

When she said nothing, I glanced over, and she quickly turned her head out the window. I quirked a brow but said nothing about that.

"Toronto is a mecca for food." I continued. "Thai, Chinese, Italian, Jamaican, Filipino—McDonalds?"

Tianna laughed out loud at that. "Thai, please."

"Good." I told her. "I figured we could swing by the last place Joseph lived before we headed home."

"Now? Is this the best time to go calling on people?"

"I find the night is when shady people do all their best work." I told her. "Besides, if we don't want to be seen, darkness is the best cover."

Tianna said nothing to that.

Church and Wellesley was a colourful intersection. Aside from the beginning of the LGBT hub in the city, it had a crosswalk painted in the colours of the rainbow flag.

The buildings were lit up, people walked back and

forth. Periodically, a bar door opened, and the dull throb of music pulsed outside in the air.

Mom and pop stores sat, windows darkened, signs drawn in, while restaurants welcomed patrons in and out.

When I eased the truck into a parking spot at the apartment, I arched a brow. I wasn't sure how Joseph even got the place with his credit and nothing to hold just in case. It was a luxury spot, one that had a night guard and a front desk.

Getting in would be a lot more problematic than I thought.

"This is not going to be easy." I muttered, looking around, trying to find a different way in.

"Um—" She started rummaging through her purse. "Will this help?"

I arched a brow. "You have his FOB in your purse?"

"It's the same purse I brought to pick up his body." She confided. "I haven't had a chance to switch back to my regular one."

At my age, I'd given up trying to solve the mystery of women and their handbags. I merely shrugged and climbed from the truck.

The door was locked at a certain hour—according to the writing on the glass. We had to access the lobby using the security card. When she swiped it, the red light turned green and the door clicked. We entered and headed straight for a bank of elevators on the far side.

"Evening Ms. Sharp." The guard called.

She turned and offered him a smile, but we didn't stop until we were in the lift.

"How did he know who I was?" She turned, fear in her eyes.

"You've never been here before?"

Tianna shook her head. "I came to Toronto, headed straight to the police station. They took me to the morgue and that was that."

"Are you sure? Think back to that time."

"No!" She stressed. "Like I said, the police station and the morgue."

"It could be when you swipe the card it logs the name on the screen." I began going through the possibilities inside my head. "It is, after all, a security card."

"Why would my name be on the card?" She rationalized. "I don't own this property. It's Joe's."

"This makes no sense." I pulled my cell out to make a call. "Hex."

"I'm here." She answered promptly.

"Pick up my location." I told her as Tianna swiped the FOB once more to let us into the actual unit. "I need to you into their system. Look for any references to a Tianna Sharp or a Joseph Sharp. Then I want you to tell me who owns unit 2701."

"When do you need this by?"

"Last month."

"On it." She replied then hung up.

"You think something is wrong?" Tianna asked, looking around as if she was afraid to touch anything.

"Don't you?" I stepped around her and began looking. "That guard knew who you were without you having been here. The only way I'm thinking he knows is if he was really good friends with Joseph to have seen your picture or the card told him that you were Tianna Sharp. Either way, I need to know so I can figure out how that'll affect us."

Leaving fingerprints was at the forefront of my mind. I tried not touching much of anything. I didn't have to touch things to be able to read if something was hinky. The exterior of the unit was immaculate. Joseph's bedroom—not so much.

It was as if someone had been looking for some-thing. "Tianna?"

She darted in and gasped. "Joseph was a lot of things—but messy wasn't one of them."

"Someone was in here." I used the back of a knuckle to flip over a frame. "Whatever they were looking for, they didn't find it."

"How do you know?"

"If they'd found it, they wouldn't have come for you." I used the foot of my boot to ease a box out of the way on the floor then hunched down to inspect the powder that spilled from it. "Criminals are not only stupid, they're lazy. They tackle the easiest things first, then they branch out. This would have been the first place they would have looked."

"Shit."

I spared her a glance and returned my gaze to the box. Hex called me back then and I frowned. "Talk to me, beautiful."

"I have bad news, worse news."

"What's the bad news?"

"The bad news is, Tianna Sharp is on the ownership for the condo. I couldn't find a Joseph." She reported.

"And the worse news?"

"The security at the front desk is most likely dead and you have in coming."

"Most likely?" I questioned.

"Um—he's slumped over his keyboard—on his face."

Before I could react, someone knocked at the door.

"I'll get it." Tianna told me.

I grabbed her arm. "Don't get that."

"Why not? They could know Joseph."

"And do you really want to talk to anyone who knew your brother right now?" I snapped. "No one knew we were coming here. That means, anyone knocking on that door, is trouble."

Whoever was outside had become rather insistent. The knocking growing louder with each thud.

"Open the door." I told her, following her toward it.

I took up my position on the other side of the door. Once she opened it, two men barged in.

As I suspected, they were too preoccupied with her to notice me. When the second man closed the door, I grabbed him, spun him around and slammed his face as hard as my two hundred pounds of muscle could manage.

When I released him, he slumped to the floor, half his face caved in and bloody.

The other man turned at the commotion and Tianna got him against the back of the head with a bronze statute that had been sitting on a small table against the wall.

He hit the floor and the statue slipped from her fingers, landing on the man's chest.

"Um." She squeaked as I rummaged through the men's pockets to see if I could find anything.

Aside from the guns and phones, they had nothing—no identification, no wallets, nothing.

They did however have tattoos—and when I pushed up their sleeves, I wanted to be sick.

"Now is not the time to pick their pockets!" Tianna cried.

I ignored her outburst. But spared her a look up. She was shaking and I knew if we didn't get out of there immediately, I'd have to carry her.

"It's okay." I rose and took her hand, tugging her toward me.

Before easing into the hallway, I checked both ways then lead her out into the hall and toward the stairs while holding down the number nine on my phone. It did its little song before Hex's voice filled my ear.

"What's up?"

"We have trouble." I told her.

"Don't worry," She said. "I took care of the cameras except one. I needed eyes in the lobby. "You're clear as of right now. Go down one more floor. I've activated an elevator for you."

"You're a doll."

We scrambled down the stairs to the floor Hex told us and the elevator was sitting there waiting. We stumbled in and the door immediately closed. The lift carried us downward to the lobby and we darted out to find my truck.

"I have some more clean up to do, then you can send me what you find for me to narrow down the ocean I'm swimming in right now." Hex instructed.

"Roger." I replied.

I stopped to pick up some food and by the time we arrived at my place, she'd calmed down somewhat but Tianna was still trembling a little. I sat her down, poured her a shot of whiskey and handed it to her.

Tianna sniffed and tried giving it back. "Too strong."

"Trust me, you need this." I pushed the crystal glass back to her. "Drink."

The hesitation was ripe in her troubled eyes, but she used her free hand to hold her nose then tossed back the drink. I wasn't sure why she held her nose, but whatever worked for her. She winced, set the glass on the island then released her nose.

"Do you want to talk about what happened back there?" I asked her.

"Could I take a shower first?" Tianna asked. "The water should help with the shaking."

I wasn't sure her surrounding herself with water in this state would be healthy. But I wasn't leaving, so if anything, I'd be around. I nodded and brought her up the stairs.

It took some time to show her around then to the room she'd be using until we figured out what the next step was. Leaving her in the bathroom, I hurried to my room and dug through my closet and came up with a t-shirt. It should be big enough on her that she could use it as a nightgown until I could get her somewhere to pick up some clothes.

I brought it back to her then went into my office. I worked until she was calling my name. Closing my laptop, I joined her to eat something.

"How do you know Montana?" She asked. "I mean, you're Canadian, right?"

"Right." I replied simply.

"Okay…did you work together?"

"Something like that."

She sighed loudly. "Fine, I get it. I can take a hint."

"Tell me about your brother—what was he into? What were his favorite scams?"

"I don't know why you'd think I know much about him." She mumbled. "He only came by when he wanted something."

"Okay, what did he usually want?"

"Money."

"Maybe that's how he bought the condo." I speculated.

"It wasn't never a lot of money." She shrugged. "Not luxury condo money."

"Yes, but a little adds up to a lot." I finished my food and set the plate down. "Think about it. You take a dollar here, a dollar there. No one misses that amount, usually."

She sighed.

I stopped speaking. She stopped eating.

Eventually, I talked her into getting some sleep and called Juju "Hex" Takimura.

Her face popped up on the screen while she scooped rice into her mouth with a pair of chopsticks. She chewed, swallowed then smiled at me.

"Hermes." Juju leaned forward. "You're up late. Super freaky fun times?"

"I wouldn't be calling you during that, Hex, trust me."

She giggled. "I take it you want to know what I've found out?"

I nodded and picked up my plate.

"Well." Hex sipped from a drink, set it down and began typing. "Her brother has no real money, property, nothing. He has a small bank account—"

"When you say small…"

"There's fourteen dollars and twenty-seven scents in it." She replied. "His cell phone has been disconnected due to nonpayment. All the legal money he's ever had was transferred from his sister. Sometimes there's a swell in his account that didn't come from her. But random grand Cayman island transfers."

"Who owns those accounts?"

"Numbered companies." She replied. "And those don't really need a person's name so—"

"Dead end."

"Precisely." She told me.

"How about a vehicle."

"It was totalled a week before he died."

I sighed. "Okay. Any luck tracking his movements the weeks before his death?"

"He has no credit cards in his name." Hex replied. "But the week before he died, he spent a lot of time at a hotel on Gerard Street called the Hideaway."

I grunted. Typical man—I knew the place well. After returning from the military, on my off time from the company, I would help a friend of mine out. He was a cop, needed undercover eyes—it was off the books. I wasn't a cop, and I didn't want to be labeled as an informant. The truth was, I had a particular set of skills that came in handy for him.

"What was he doing there?" I asked.

"What do people do at a place called the Hideaway?"

"I'm surprise that place has a computer system." I left the screen to get a drink. "Everything about the Hideaway seems above board. I mean, if the freaky shit they did there was out in the open it would have been shut down years ago. But what the owners don't see, they don't know—right?"

I went back to my seat and flopped into the chair. "Right."

"Other than that, he was pretty much off grid." Hex shrugged. "People don't realize how much others can tell about them through their credit card records."

I rubbed my eyes. "But he didn't have a credit card."

"No." Hex sighed. "For a hacker, that's like chasing a ghost."

"I've never heard you talked like this before, Hex." I leaned in. "Are you saying it's impossible?"

If looks could kill.

"Don't be a dick." She grumbled. "I'm not saying it's not impossible—just very, very frustrating. I have a software trying to do a little facial rec on him. It's going to be rough but at least we'll have something of a map."

"I'm going to try getting some shut-eye." I told her, knowing it would have to be a miracle if I got any sleep. "Let me know what you find."

I woke up with the sunlight in my face, my body tangled in a comfortable blanket and one leg sticking out at the bottom. For a second, I didn't know where I was, and I didn't care. The blanket was soft and warm and sensual against my skin. The pillows were the right firmness, and the mattress held my body like a lover.

Then it all crashed down on me.

My brother was dead and the night before I watched the man who was supposed to protect me kill a man by crushing his face.

My heart raced.

Hermes was the trickster—but from what I remembered he could be volatile if tested. They'd chosen the perfect callsign for Maksim.

A part of me was terrified of Hermes.

Another part of me was hot for him.

I frowned.

So, he looked like everything from every, single one of my wet dreams.

So, I had a thing for men with large hands.

So, his icy blue eyes were sexy enough to look through my soul.

I sighed.

Frustrated, I covered my face, wanting a few more seconds before I venture back into the breach.

When I rolled over to stare at the back of my closed door and to check out the room. A bag, seemingly from a high-end clothing store, sat on a plus chair close to the bookshelf.

Was that there last night?

Curious, I scrambled from bed and rushed over to check it out. A note was stuck to the outside and I pulled it off.

Get dressed and come out for breakfast." Time's-a-wastin'—Hermes.

Excited, I looked inside and began removing things. The jeans, and tops weren't surprising. When my hand hit the bone of a brassier, my jaw dropped. "Um, what-in-the…" The first bra was black, a zipper at the front. Ever since I was a little girl, I loved having those kinds of bras. The second was a deep blue, hooked at the back but beautiful. The third was pink, covered in cherry blossom buds.

I held it up to check the tag and realized they

were perfect. Still, reeling, I stuck my hand in again to find a couple pairs of panties.

I choked.

Did this man go out and buy me intimates?

Even as I washed in the shower, I couldn't get over it.

Eventually, I entered the living space to find him eating scrambled eggs and staring intently at his laptop's screen.

"I wonder what they were doing there?" Montana's voice escaped the screen. "I mean, there couldn't have been a way to know she was coming. We haven't told anyone."

"Maybe the guard did." Hermes looked over at me as he replied.

Something played about his eyes. I tried figuring out what it was, but he looked back at the screen. Embarrassed, I sat beside Hermes and waved at Montana.

"How are you holding up?" Montana asked.

"I'm still standing." I offered a smile. "I'm okay."

"Babe?" A woman called from off screen. "I'm heading out."

She stepped into view to kiss him "Don't forget, Emma wants you to take her to the park. I tried and she wants you."

"I won't forget." He grinned impishly and kissed her again.

"You're quite proud of yourself, aren't you?" Sadie asked.

Montana laughed. "Of course, I am."

"And if she comes home covered in mud, you're washing her."

"It happened once!" Montana laughed. "But I can't make any promises it won't again. If we see a puddle it shall be jumped in."

Sadie laughed—even her laugh was perfect.

I wanted to hate her. But how could I? If Montana fell for her that meant she was an angel.

I was sick to my stomach.

There was no way my soul would let me dislike her. I needed forgiveness and there was no hate in forgiveness.

A pain pulsed in my chest causing me to wince.

"You okay?" Montana asked.

His questioned cause Hermes to glance over at me and that also brought Sadie's eyes to me for the first time since she stepped into view.

"I'm good." I squeaked.

"Hey Hermes—" Sadie greeted him with a smile.

"Hey Sadie. You be safe." Hermes told her. "Don't take candy from strangers."

"But strangers have the best candy!" She pouted.

"You've been with Montana too long." Hermes teased.

She winked at him, offered me a curt nod then kissed Montana again and turned to leave.

Montana smacked her rump playfully and she squealed.

"Hank Patterson! You have company!" But she giggled while leaving. "You two behave yourselves! And Emma. Park."

"Aye ay captain!" Montana called.

I wanted the floor to open up and swallow me.

If Montana realized, he said nothing. Instead, he and Hermes continued speaking about my trouble and I wandered off to grab some food. When I returned, Montana was gone, and Hermes was slamming the bottom of his handgun into his palm.

"Why do you need a gun?" I asked.

Hermes stared at me. "Well, when we go after the very bad men—I might need this so you don't wind up dead."

"Smart-ass." I muttered. "Thanks for the clothes but you didn't really have to get me panties and bras."

"Got it. Next time, you prefer to go commando." He smirked. "But I figured you wouldn't want to walk around braless—it gets cold and you'd be cutting holes through things."

"Oh my God!" I spat softly. "You're an asshole."

He laughed while strapping a holster around one massive thigh and dropping the gun into it. "Thank you."

"It wasn't a compliment."

He said nothing but the grin on his face told me he'd won this argument. Even though I didn't see how, I lifted my chin. "How do you know my bra-size?"

"Despite what you think, Tianna, I'm not a virgin. I've been with women. I've touched them in ways to make you blush."

My cheeks were on fire. Thankfully, with my skin-colour, he probably couldn't tell. Instead of bowing my head like I would usually do, I steeled my spine and kept my chin up. "I didn't think you were a virgin. You probably sleep with everything on two feet."

"Maybe." He scoffed. "But you don't have to worry. I won't be sleeping with you."

The sharp pain of an arrow crashed into my chest and the steel in my spine disintegrated as my chin fell. "Thanks for the clothes—I'll pay you back."

"That's not necessary."

"You're helping me with this." I told him. "I don't want to take your money too. I mean, it wouldn't feel right."

"When this is over." Hermes pushed to his over-powering height. "You can take me out for a drink."

"Are you asking me out on a date?"

Hermes smirked at me and I had to press my thighs together again. Each time the right corner of his lips tugged upward, my body heated, and I lose track of my thoughts.

"Shut up." I said stupidly, like a child who couldn't think of a comeback fast enough.

Hermes exited the room, his masculine laughter drifting in on me.

I moaned.

If he kept being that damn sexy, I wouldn't be making it.

Eating was the last thing on my mind then. I brought the rest of my food back to the kitchen and used a bowl to cover the plate. I poured myself a cup of coffee from his fancy maker and sipped without adding anything. I needed the caffeine to hit my soul before I strangle this man.

I barely had time to finish my anti-murder juice before he was back. He herded me out a side door, down a winding staircase that dropped us in the middle of a large garage. The room must have been the basement to the massive house.

"Is all this yours?" I turned, looking from one car to another. A midnight black one caught my attention and I gasped. "The Supernatural car!"

Hermes laughed. "You don't have to say it in that kind of a whisper."

"Yes, I do!" I drew close to it. "You have no idea how many fantasies I have about this car."

"Oh?" Hermes was close to my ear. "Tell me more."

I opened my mouth to reply then caught myself. "No!" I sputtered. "Pick a car and let's go."

Hermes laughed. "What does a woman like you fantasize about, Tianna?"

I couldn't reply. If I had, I would definitely say something to embarrass myself and couldn't take back. His beautiful eyes made me want to tell him everything, they made me want to give him anything, hold nothing back. There was something about the way I felt when he looked at me that made me think all kinds of taboo things.

He settled for a Hellcat Widebody Redeye with the red key. My brother had explained what that meant a long time ago, but I couldn't remember why the key was red.

I dragged on my seatbelt and moaned as the car roared to life.

Leaving the quiet of Scarborough, as Hermes explained, we headed into the downtown core. He stopped so I could pick things up for my hair, and once I was in the car again, he continued to a hotel that looked as though it was in the wrong place.

It was at least twenty minutes from any main intersection, and aside from a small convenience store, there wasn't anything else around it worth mentioning.

The word *Hideaway* stood out in a strange, tacky blue light font. It rubbed me the wrong way and I didn't want to go in there.

"Do you have a picture of you and Joseph together?"

I pulled one up on my phone.

"I need you to put your phone on airplane mode." I told her.

"Because of—oh—right! Sorry." I quickly did as he said.

"When we go in, you ask if they know Joseph." He explained. "They'll have more sympathy for you since you're his sister. They may not know he's dead, so don't bring that up. Keep it simply. You're his sister and you're trying to find him. Got it?"

I nodded, taking deep, cleansing breaths. "I can do this."

We climbed from the car and I watched as he walked around, light trench coat dropping just by his knees, his combat boots laced tightly, and his jeans painted to his very sexy thighs. I tried not to focus on wanting him, on crushing on him, but it was better than freaking out about what we were walking into.

I walked with him toward the building and he reached around me to open the door. Stepping in, I expected tacky. But the lobby was like a luxury hotel. Plants in the corners, pristine floors, luxury chairs—I figured when rich folks wanted to cheat on their spouses, they wanted to do it in style.

Swallowing the nervous lump in my throat, I lifted my chin, and we made our way up to the front desk and I flashed the picture. "Have you seen this man?" I asked.

The clerk stared at me, then frowned.

"We're not cops." Hermes told him.

"This man is my brother." I pushed. "I just wanted to know if you've seen him. I'm going into every business on this street because someone told me he was in this area lately."

"Let me see the picture again," The man said.

I quickly did as he asked, and he nodded. "I know him. I mean I don't really know him, but he used to come in here."

"Have you seen him lately?" Hermes asked.

"No. Not for a few weeks, I think." The man replied. "He usually comes in with a blond. Come to think of it, I haven't seen either of them in a while."

I sighed. When I looked over at Hermes, he seemed deep in thought.

"Could we see the room he used to stay in?" I asked.

"I really shouldn't let anyone in there."

"Okay, how about I book the room for the night?" I asked him. "If it's free."

"What's the guy's name?" The clerk asked.

"Sharp, Joseph Sharp." I replied.

He tapped away at his computer then looked up. "Name?"

"Karina Sharp." I lied.

I paid the fee for one night in cash and was sent up to the room with Hermes in tow. The elevator brought us up to the tenth floor and I tapped the key against the access box.

Once inside, I could instantly tell the room had

been cleaned. The smell of disinfectant was so strong, I had to cover my nose and mouth with a hand.

"Strange," Hermes said as he peeked out the window then turned his attention to the large space.

I wasn't sure what we were looking for. Why I thought we'd be able to find anything in the space was beyond me. It'd been a while since Joseph had used it. There was no telling how many people had checked into it since then, how many times it had been cleaned.

We checked everything—found nothing.

"Who do you think the woman was?" I asked Hermes while he peered into the bathroom.

"Girlfriend, lover, friend?"

"Why would they need to come to this place?" I asked. "I mean, if you're dating, you're dating."

"Maybe she was married."

"My brother wouldn't be dating a married woman." I huffed.

Hermes said nothing to that. But when I looked over at him, I could tell he wanted to say something. When he didn't, I exhaled and looked under the bed one more time. Usually, when people cleaned, underneath the bed wasn't high on their list.

Pulling out my phone, I turned on the flashlight and used it to see better. The space there was relatively clean except for one thing that glinted in the light.

"Um—Hermes?"

"Yeah?"

"There's something under here." I told him.

There was a grunt, then a creak and the bed lifted in the air. Stunned, I looked up to see Hermes had palmed the foot of the bed and had lifted the entire thing up so I could reach the thing that had caught my attention.

Shaking myself, I rushed forward, grabbed it and rolled away so he could put the bed back. He gritted his teeth and hunched down like a power lifter. Once the bed was safely down, I looked in my hands to see what I'd grabbed. "It's a chip of some sort."

"Here, let me see." Hermes extended a large palm. "It's a chip—from a phone."

"It could be from them or any number of places." I told him.

"We should go." Hermes told me. "We'll check it. But for now, we should get out of here."

Getting out of the hotel was easy enough. We climbed into the truck but the moment we got in, Hermes was glancing in his rear-view mirror.

"What's the matter?"

"Nothing." He offered a smile. "Seatbelt."

We stopped to pick up some food, and all the way he kept checking behind us.

"Okay, what's wrong?" I insisted. "And don't tell me nothing."

He frowned. "We're being followed."

"Are you sure?" I shifted to look back, but he grabbed my arm.

"Don't look back!" Hermes snapped.

He checked his mirrors, switched lanes and sped up. I leaned toward him to look into the sideview mirror to find a black car sticking to our tail. I muttered a profanity under my breath.

The chase carried us through the downtown core, zig-zagging through traffic with horns blaring at us. We zoomed around streetcars, along side streets to avoid traffic.

The Hellcat handled like a dream, taking corners perfectly. The other vehicle barely kept up, but it was there, even as Hermes turned down an alley with graffiti on both sides of the walls.

Then the bullets rained.

I screamed.

"Keep your head down!" Hermes hollered, slamming his foot down on the gas, propelling the vehicle faster.

But there wasn't much space, especially with the restriction of the seatbelt. With bullets whizzing around, I pushed, forcing the seatbelt to expand then used my arms to cover my head.

The madness went on for a while until the momentum of the vehicle switched. There was a low screeching then a bang. The car jolted to a stop and I looked up in time to see Hermes pulling the gun from his holster and shoving from the car.

"Stay here." He ordered. "Keep your head down."

"What? You can't just…"

"Not the time, Tianna." He barked.

He slammed the door and I watched as his body went from angry at me to war-mode. There was a way soldiers carried themselves in certain situations that told me they were prepared. It was only then I realized the car that had been chasing us had flipped.

Hermes hefted his gun, holding it in his right hand with his left hand, cupping it. He moved quickly for his size, covering space to the car rapidly. When he was close, a bullet shattered the windshield of the overturned car. Hermes sidestepped and fired two shots through the glass.

He eased around the side, while pushing his foot through the window. He disappeared and I stopped breathing.

There was an eternity between him disappearing and popping up again. This time, dragging a body away from the vehicle then dropping it. The man on the ground tried reaching for him but Hermes merely stepped on his hand. The two of them were speaking to each other. I was too far to hear what was being said.

Again, the man lunged for Hermes who set a heavy foot in the center of his chest and planted him back on the ground.

The far-a-way wail of sirens caught my attention and I groaned. I unclipped my seatbelt, dragged myself across the middle and fell into the driver's seat. I started the ignition and flipped a U-turn. I sped to where he was, just as the sirens grew louder and began coming up the street toward the water's edge.

"Get in!" I yelled, shoving the passenger side open. "Come on!"

Hermes holstered his weapon and tossed his body into the seat.

I sped in the opposite direction of the police car, glancing back periodically to see if we were being followed. While I tried outrunning a police cruiser, Hermes put on his seatbelt, and reached forward to press a button. A whirring at the front of the car and the back caught my attention and I freaked and pressed my foot down on the gas.

"Shit! Now, I'm running from the cops?" I blurted out. "How did that even happen? I can't go to jail! I don't wanna go to jail! I like my life the way it is!"

"Tianna?"

"He's dead and he's still messing with my life!" I continued as if he hadn't spoken. "I buried him, and he just won't stop! Now I'm running from the cops!"

"Tianna!"

"What!" I snapped. "Don't you yell at me!"

"Make the next left." He ordered, lifting his phone to his ear. "Then the first right you come to."

I did as he said and continued, the Hellcat blowing by things like a rocket.

"Hex." Hermes called. "Listen, I need an out. Moving in the Hellcat—right, you got me? Okay. Perfect."

"I'm going to need you to twist the steering to the right and slam on the brakes, okay?" Hermes told me.

"What? I'm not trying to get killed!"

"Just arrested."

"Shit!" I swore. "Okay, when…"

He was staring in the rear-view mirror so intently, I wasn't sure he heard me.

"Hermes!"

"Now!" He shouted.

Holding my breath, I did as he instructed. The car whipped around, tires screaming then jarred to a stop.

"Slam on the gas! Go!" Hermes ordered.

The black car zoomed by the cop car and in my rear-view mirror I watched as they slammed into the guardrail.

"No…"

"They'll be fine." He told me. "They have a rammer on the front of the car. They'll be banged up but fine."

In that moment, I hated my brother. Because of him I had idiots trying to grab me, threatening my life. Now, I've brought Hermes into this mess while getting cops hurt. I wanted to cry—I wanted to curl into the insignificant ball I'd become and sob until the world ended.

I had always been my brother's keeper. Even before we lost our parents, and the rest of the family turned their backs on us. I'd taken it on my shoulders to take care of Joseph.

Giving him anything he wanted may not have been the best move—I saw that now.

The strange thing was, I probably wouldn't live long enough to learn my lesson.

Weren't the fates grand?

MAKSIM "HERMES" DEMIDOV

TIANNA CONTROLLED my sports car like she belonged behind the wheel. Some women would have panicked when the bullets started flying. It seemed she'd taken her moment to freak out—then got down to business.

My kind of woman.

I coughed and rubbed my eyes.

Where the hell did that thought come from?

I had her pull the hellcat into the garage and the moment the door closed and she turned off the engine, She flopped back into the seat, her knuckles still clutching the steering, so tight, her knuckles lost their colour.

"Tianna?" I whispered softly. "Anna, sweetheart?"

Some of her hair had come loose from the pony-tail and was blocking her face. I reached across to tuck the strands closest to me behind her ear. She jerked to look at me as though she'd forgotten I was there.

"Shhh." I whispered. "It's okay. Come on, let me get you inside."

She stared at me, wide-eyed.

I scrambled from the vehicle and went around to her side. When I opened the door, she dropped the keys into my palm, and I helped her to her feet. At first her knees wobbled, and she gripped her hips to steady her.

I scooped her into my arms and carried her into the house. After setting her on the sofa, I knelt beside her to check her eyes to see if she was going into shock. So far, she seemed fine but rattled I left her for a moment for something to drink.

I settled for two shots of tequila but an hour later, Tianna still hadn't said anything to me. The silence didn't worry me—what concerned me was her shaking. She couldn't seem to stop shaking. When I poured her the first shot, she tossed it back without lime or salt. The second one disappeared as well, and she set the shot glass on the island. She lifted her hands to watch her palms.

The shots had done nothing.

She was still trembling.

It perplexed me because I didn't know if I should brace myself for her to go into shock or take my head off.

Either way, she was not happy with today's turn of events and couldn't say I blame her.

I peeled my shirt over my head and flung it to the laundry basket in between the dresser and the bathroom door, then began digging for another when a loud thump caught my attention.

I ran from my room. She wasn't in the bedroom and when I saw the bathroom door was closed, my heart did a strange lurch.

Had she fallen over?

Was she in the tub? The water was running so that could be it. Rushing over, I knocked. "Tianna?" I called. "I heard a sound. Are you okay?"

But all I heard was her sobbing. Worried, I opened the door a crack. "Are you um…I'm coming in."

When I did face her, she was fully clothed and standing under the shower. The water had soaked through her hair, pressing the strands to the sides of her head and down her face.

I climbed into the tub with her and framed her face with my palms. "Talk to me, Tianna. Tell me what's going on in your mind."

"I-I don't know." She stammered. "I don't know. All I know is I want all of this to be over. I can't stop shaking—it's been over an hour and my body is still doing this mess!"

Tianna held her hand up to show me. "Can you believe this? What the hell kind of weakling—"

"Weak?" I tilted my head. "Tianna you climbed behind the wheel and got us out of there. Another woman would have freaked out. She would be screaming as the shots flew."

"Don't kid yourself—I did scream. You probably didn't hear me."

I smiled. "Okay, once. What I'm trying to say is you did good today."

"I just wish I could stop shaking. How comes you aren't a mess too?"

"Years of conditioning." I told her. "Besides, you wouldn't want a bodyguard who gets spooked easy, am I right?"

"You got a point there."

Exhaling, I drew her into my chest, tangled the fingers of one hand in her wet hair and held her cheek to my shoulder. When she wrapped her arms around my body, she sighed and relaxed into me.

"It's okay." I kissed the side of her head.

"It won't ever be okay again—not really," she said. "Unless you have a time machine in your bedroom somewhere."

I chuckled.

The asshole in me wanted to make a joke about what was in my bedroom, but I swallowed the joke. "We're going to figure this out and then you can go home again."

Years ago, I lost any sort of gentleness in me—at least I thought I had. It was eaten away by the war and the faces of dead strangers. But having her close and hurting did something to me. It brought back memories of a time when I was at least a little human.

"We should get you dried off." My voice cracked as I reached around her to turn off the water.

"I actually want to get a shower." She sniffled then sneezed.

"This time, maybe turn on the hot water?"

She grinned impishly. "Sorry. Was trying to fix a problem before the depression kicked in."

I smirked. "A problem? Do I make you horny, baby?"

She smacked my arm. "Are you always this filthy?"

"Do you really wanna know?" I dropped my voice. "I always thought a question like that shouldn't be answered with words. Actions speak way louder."

Tianna trembled in my arms then pointed to the door. "Go." She laughed. "I need to shower."

Groaning, I climbed from the tub, grabbed a couple of the towels, and exited the bathroom. I dried the excess water from my jeans then peeled it off. After wrapping a towel around my hips, I turned to look at the closed door.

As I stared, I knew I wouldn't be able to fall asleep ever again. I knew what her body felt like, pressing into mine as intimately as I could get without being slapped. Her curves pressed into me was the closest

I'd been to heaven and I didn't want to go back to reality.

I wanted to stay in that tub, cold water chilling me to the bone with her hot frame warming me like no fire could.

Yes, I'd wanted to kiss her. But what kind of man would that make me? She was in pain—kissing her would have been the absolute wrong thing to do in that moment.

Besides, the way she looked at Montana drove the message home loud and clear.

Tianna wasn't over him.

Even though Montana was now with someone, I knew she still hungered for him. There was a time I would have done anything to have a woman look at me like that—like I was the best thing in their world, like I was the sexiest man alive.

But having my heart ripped out of my chest cured me of those dreams. Women were nothing but trouble. Besides, this was a favour to Montana. The last thing I should be doing was getting distracted by a pretty face, curves deeper than a mountain road and an ass I knew would feel magnificent in my palms.

We didn't have much time. Whatever we were doing, we had to do it now and get the hell out of dodge.

While I waited for her, I slipped my phone's chip out and pushed in the one we found at the hotel. The cell came on and opened up to the locked screen with a picture of Joseph and, who I assumed was Tianna. They were young—in their late teens. That was probably the last picture they took together where Tianna didn't want to kick his ass to another dimension.

But other than the front screen, the chip was locked. Joseph hadn't been smart enough to encrypt it. That meant, he either paid someone to do it, or the chip came that way and he'd gotten someone to hack it.

I called Hex and was told I had to bring it to her. The way it was set up, there was nothing she could do remotely.

"I thought you were a genius. What happened to that?"

"You know how you can't really make a woman come unless you're touching her?"

I quirked a brow. "Say what? You do know there's other ways of…"

"Don't lip me, Pan."

I growled. She knew when she called me that it irritated me.

"Down boy." She teased.

I grunted.

"In all seriousness." She brought my mind back to the task at hand. "I need to put it into a special piece of equipment to work on it."

"All right. Let me work on some stuff then I'll bring me the chip a little later."

She agreed and I hung up then replaced my chip

and dropped Joseph's into a second phone I had. I shoved it into my back pocket just as Tianna entered the room. Staring was rude—I had to remember that. But when my eyes were speaking with my brain, I rose and busied myself sharing her some food so we could sit down and talk.

"So, Joseph pissed off these Owls?" Tianna asked.

"Maybe." I told her.

"Maybe?" She frowned. "Which is it?"

"The Owls make most of their money by hiring themselves out for jobs."

"So, what you're saying is, we can't tell yet if they are the ones after me or if they're working for someone else who's after me?"

I nodded.

"Fan-fucking-tastic."

"The two guys who attacked us at the condo are a part of the gang. The two in the car we ran from today are members as well."

"Did they tell you what Joseph did?"

"Well, according to them," I said. "They are looking for the chip we found at the hotel. They don't know we have it. They're hoping he told you and we would lead them to where it is or who has it. So, they were basically ordered to follow us until we do or until the boss gets impatient."

"He can get as impatient as he wants." Tianna told me. "He's not getting that chip. He killed my brother over it and I'm going to use it to bury the son-of-a-bitch."

Her anger turned me on.

Damn it!

"And no word of what's on the chip?" "Tianna asked. "At least I'll know what was so damn important to take a life and attack us."

I shrugged. "He was about to tell me when you turned into Dominic Toretto and demanded I get in the car."

All I received from her for my attempt at a joke was a cold, expressionless stare. "Did you try seeing what was on the chip?"

"When you were in the shower."

"And?"

"It's encrypted."

"What?" She snapped. "What in the—how in the actual hell would he have known how to do that? This was the idiot who failed grades nine, ten and eleven math. You're telling me, the guy who called me because he did know where the bold function was in Words, encrypted a chip? How would he learn how to—you know what? Whatever. I don't care."

"Tianna…"

"I don't care." Tianna offered a one shoulder shrug. "We go one step forward three steps back. Joseph has been an asshole one too many times and now it's coming back to haunt me."

"Don't worry. I know this is hard—"

"Then stop telling me not to worry." She snapped. "I'm going to die because my brother didn't love me enough to think how this would blow back to me."

Then it hit me. "How would they know to come for you?" I muttered.

"Someone told them?"

"Yeah." I scratched the back of my neck with the nail of my thumb. "I mean—you were in a whole other country. This could mean your brother had this chip since he came to you to ask for money."

"That's also a possibility

I knew we should be going. We'd packed overnight bags and would be staying somewhere else. Sure, the hellcat had a trick paintjob, but there were very few people in Toronto—hell, in all of Canada— with a car like the demon cat.

"I need your phone." I told her.

It seemed the fight had died in her. Instead of arguing like I thought she would, Tianna handed the cell over the focused on rooting through the fridge for bottles of water. When she walked by me, I turned with an arched brow.

"Tianna?"

"Yeah?"

"I'm going to leave you with a friend to go see Hex." I explained.

"Why can't I go with you?"

"Because Hex has a thing about strangers

knowing where she is at any given time." I replied. "I have to bring her the phone chip."

"Why? If it's encrypted what's she going to do?"

"She has ways of getting into things that we don't have."

"In other words, she's a hacker?"

I rubbed my neck. "The less you know, the better." Want to get a drink before we head out?"

"No. I don't think you have anything strong enough to get rid of what I'm feeling right now." She picked up her bag and headed for the door leading to the garage.

This time, I pulled out one of the trucks and we were on our way. She seemed to have wanted silence and I used the time to try and put things right in my head.

HERMES' friend was nice enough—I supposed. She was pretty and Hermes greeted her by catching her against his massive chest and twirled her around. She'd tossed her head back and laughed. For some reason I found myself wanting to dislike her.

Jealousy?

"I'm not feeling so good." I lied.

"There is a space upstairs," Echo said. "Come on, once you say goodbye to Hermes, I can take you up and you can lay down for a bit."

I frowned. She hadn't been rude about it as I'd expected. All the way to the room, I frowned at the way I had been thinking. I barely knew Hermes.

I had no reason to be jealous.

"Bathroom is over there." She pointed. "I'll check on you later—let me know if you need anything."

"Thank you." I managed.

Echo walked by me and everything about her said she was the kind of woman I should be but never would be. The door clicked behind her and I pressed my lips into a thin line. After getting over my reaction to her, I glanced around. It wasn't super elegant, but it was comfortable. The bed was backed up to the large window and she'd draped see through curtains over the four-poster bed. It was the kind of room I wanted when I was a kid.

Being in the room by myself was beginning to drive me crazy. Nothing I did was comfortable.

Sitting was becoming an issue.

I couldn't sit. I couldn't stand. I tried lying down but couldn't do that either. There were so many things going through my mind. I worry that Hermes was now digging into something that someone was willing to kill to get back. My safety suddenly wasn't as important. I wanted to call this whole thing off and face what was coming alone.

Leaving the room, I wandered down a corridor and let myself through an ornate door. Continuing down the stairs, I stepped through into the *Crosshairs* bar. The woman Hermes had called Echo, looked up at me and smiled. She was beautiful with a body any woman would kill for. Echo wasn't skinny, but she was fit, curves in all the right places. Her dark hair had been shaved down, natural. I remembered her eyes were brown, bright—filled with a kind of content light I envied her for.

"Hey." I wrapped my arms around myself.

"How was your nap?" She asked.

"I didn't get much of a one." I admitted, taking a seat to watch her clean up. "I think I'm a little more rattled than I thought. I don't want Hermes to worry."

"Good luck with that." She smiled.

"What's your actual name?" I asked her.

"What's the matter?" She asked. "Don't I look like an Echo?"

I shrugged. "I don't think your mother would have named you Echo."

She giggled. "She didn't. Elise Parsons."

"You were military?" I asked. "I can't think of any other way you'd wind up with a nickname like Echo."

Echo chuckled. "Yes, sniper."

My eyes widened. "Really? Wow."

I glanced over my shoulder when the heavy doors opened. An elderly gentleman walked through, and I turned on my stool and hung my head.

"He'll be okay." Echo told me. "He's with Hex, who has his back like no one else. You can trust her."

"I'm not worried about Hex." I told her. "The only thing I'm worried about with her—"

"How long have you known Hermes?"

"Not long."

Echo cleared her throat, wiped a glass, and set it in the holder with the others. "But you like him."

I scoffed.

"Love is a strange thing, Tianna."

"Love?" I choked. "Hermes is a good man. I can tell—and aside from our friend in Montana, I'm not used to good men."

"Well, a bit of unsolicited advice?"

I smiled. "Why do I get the feeling that even if I said no, you're going to give it to me anyway?"

"Because I'm that bitch."

I nodded.

"You said it yourself." Echo leaned forward, resting her elbows on the bar. "You don't meet a lot of good men. When you do meet one, and there is some attraction there, you need to find out if those feelings are mutual. If they are, explore."

"This isn't a mission."

"You're right. It's life. I can agree with you that Hermes is a good man. I've been around him with enough time to tell you any woman would kill to have him in her life, her bed."

"Including you?"

"Including me. But I'm not his type." Echo explained.

"Really? Pretty, ambitious, kick-ass, is not his type? Is he gay?"

"No." Echo exhaled and stood up. "Hungry?"

I figured she didn't want to talk about it anymore. The thought of them together angered me. It shouldn't have but how could I not be a little jealous?

I knew what it felt like to being in his arms, to feel

his lips against the side of my head, his large palms, massaging my back. I love the way my heart raced as he whispered comforts to me, of feeling his heated breath on my face.

It was the first time I'd ever experienced that with a man. He'd held onto me and never once made me feel as if I owed him anything.

It was true comfort.

I exhaled loudly.

"Listen, Doll." Echo set a plate in front of me with fries and a burger.

It stunned me. I was so out of it, I didn't know she'd even left the space. I blinked and she was placing a glass bottle with vinegar along with ketchup and mayo beside the plate.

"My father would like to believe that I don't know much." Echo's voice cracked with emotions. She picked up a clean glass and the tap for soda. "But I know a few things without certainty. One, tomorrow isn't promised to anyone. That leads me into point two, life is short. You may have no idea how short— but in the military, you know. And three, love isn't always at first sight. That whole bullshit about men falling in love in eight point two seconds is just that —it's bullshit."

"What if its true?"

"You think someone can tell all the things it's taken a whole date to find out about someone in eight point two seconds?"

I shrugged. "Maybe."

"Eat." Echo placed the soda beside my plate.

"I'm serious." I drowned my fries in ketchup. "That would mean, I would have had eight point two seconds upon meeting Hermes, for him to decide I was cute enough to fall for."

"Upon?" Echo turned to smirk at me over a shoulder. "Tianna, you're giving that too much thought."

"Okay—what do you believe?"

Echo picked up a blue bottle and moved it to a lower shelf before facing me again. "I think you can be infatuated in eight point two seconds. I mean, our eyes and brains are geared toward our own version of beauty. When we see it, we want to gravitate toward it."

"Your round about way of saying love comes later." I shoved a fry into my mouth.

"Maybe." Echo inhaled deeply. Her shoulders rose to her ears before falling heavily. "Listen, life is complicated enough. Nothing in relationships are ever a sure thing. I say if both you and Hermes are willing, and he's attracted too, then you go for it."

"Like you say, I'm not his type."

Echo smiled. "Well, only one way to find out."

I sighed and grabbed another fry. "Why the vinegar?"

"I was hoping you'd try it before murdering your fries in the red stuff." Echo pointed to my plate. "Maybe next time."

I scoffed.

After I'd eaten as much as I could, I set about helping Echo behind the bar. I stayed away from the mixed drinks, but I was able to help serve customer beers and sodas. I couldn't understand how Echo loved doing this.

By the time Hermes returned, I was exhausted but couldn't remember feeling as fulfilled as spending time with Echo had made me feel. Her smile did something to put sunshine into my life and I was afraid I would lose that.

Echo brought Hermes a drink, kissed his head and walked away, leaving us in her office in the back.

"Did she do it?"

Hermes nodded. He seemed a little on edge and I rubbed my eyes.

"Joseph has information on the Brotherhood Protectors." Hermes replied.

"Why?" I asked. "He had nothing to do with Montana and the guys. Why would he have information on them? What kind of information?"

"Personal stuff—like someone was compiling the information for some reason." He replied. "They even have information on the new guy, Reaper. There were pictures that were obviously taken without the guys knowing."

"Okay..."

"Tell me how much interaction Joseph has had

with any of the guys on Montana's tea, including Montana."

"None." I shrugged. "Aside from meeting Montana once *years* ago, the two of them shouldn't have and any dealings beyond that. Maybe Joseph didn't know what was on that chip. Maybe he saw it and took it, thinking he could make some money."

"That would make sense." Hermes eyed his drink but didn't pick it up. "But there is something else here. I was thinking maybe he wanted to bring Montana down for hurting you—"

"Montana didn't hurt me." I explained. "I swear to God, this family is cursed."

"Why did the two of you break up?"

"Um—"

"Not the time to lie to me." Hermes reminded me. "I need to know if your brother took offence to that. Montana told me you ended badly, how badly?"

"I thought the Owls…"

"May have nothing to do with this." I told her. "Not really. They may just be in because someone paid them to be. Now, how did the two of you break up?"

"It wasn't like I didn't love him." I started. "He was one of the best boyfriends I ever had—hell, I was already planning our wedding. But I was young, and stupid and had no idea how a relationship really worked."

"We all had those years."

"Yeah, but not all of us loses everything for having them." I stood and walked over to the window to peer out. The view wasn't very good. Aside from a pedicured lawn a few chairs, there was a barn on the far side, sitting open. From what I could see, it was neat. "I was focused on money, on friends, on everything except him. Now, I realize all he wanted was me."

"Explain."

"I hadn't spent any time with him that week." I sighed. "It wasn't because I had anything important to do—shopping, outing with friends. All he asked was that Saturday, I spend it with him. I promised I would then, flaked. When he called me out on it, I told him I wasn't ready to be anyone's wife so he should stop trying to keep tabs on me."

"There has to be more to it than that."

"There is. I wasn't a very loyal girlfriend."

"You cheated?"

I couldn't meet his eyes. Seeing the disappointment in his gaze would kill me. "It wasn't my proudest moment. It was one time—a stupid—and that one time just took him away. I remember his eyes. I mean, I'd just blurted it out in that argument about me flaking on him. You see, I didn't even care enough to break it to him gently."

"How'd he take it?" Hermes asked. "Most men would have lost their shit."

"I wish he had." I sat again, picked up his drink

and knocked it back in one go. "Instead he looked at me as if I'd just spat in his face. Then he just walked away. So—the breakup wasn't on him and Joseph knew that."

"I'm going to have to tell them." Hermes informed me. "I mean, we don't know who else is involved in this and they have the right to know so they can protect themselves and the ones they love."

"I know." I frowned. "Another reason for Montana to hate me, so why not?"

Hermes took me to the house we'd be staying at. It was much smaller than his, but I didn't care anymore. This entire thing was getting more dangerous and I needed Montana to call off the guards.

No one else should die for this mess.

MAKSIM DEMIDOV

THE INFORMATION on the Brotherhood Protectors was extremely detailed. It was the kind of work that could have only be done by one of two sources—intelligence or an inside person. Hex had tried tracking where the information came from. The chip was American, purchased in Texas.

Other than that, there was no other way to trace where the information came from and how it got to be on the chip. I was going to wait until I had a little bit more information from Hex, but I couldn't.

Exhaling, I grabbed my phone and called Montana.

"This line is secured, right?" I asked. My cell had a few extra features, thanks to Hex.

"Always." Montana groaned.

"Were you already in bed, old man?"

"Some of us have a lady." Montana teased back. "And she wanted me in bed, if you get my drift."

I laughed. "Listen, climb out of bed for a sec. This is serious."

"Alright. Gimme a minute."

It took a moment for Montana's voice to boom over the line again. I sat around all the paperwork and began explaining to him what Hex managed to get off the chip so far. "I don't know why he has this information, but you do know it can damage the team."

"I know." Montana growled.

"We went through the thoughts, Montana." I rubbed my neck. "Did he buy this info off someone? Was he planning on selling it? Was he going to use it to come for you?"

"Joseph is an asshole." Montana told me. "He knew why his sister and I split. So, he wasn't coming for me. The more plausible explanation was he stole this info off someone and was planning on black-mailing them or selling it back to us."

I sighed. "I have the chip now. But you're going to have to vet your team—what about this new guy?"

"Reaper?" Montana scoffed. "Trust me, it's not him."

"How do you k now?" I asked without thinking.

"He's a good man, Hermes." Montana replied, his voice hard. "No—he knows what it feels like to be burned. I honestly don't think he'd do it to someone else. Besides, as the new guy, he would have been the obvious choice. I'm certain it's not him."

"You know what you have to do now, don't you?"

"Unfortunately."

"Can you spare a couple hands?" I asked him.

"Kujo."

"I'll take him. When he lands, I'll go pick him up." I promised. "In the meantime, I'll keep rattling some cages over here to figure out where this information came from. Someone went through a lot of trouble to get it together."

"Keep me posted." Montana's voice was hard. "I'll let you know Kujo's movements."

I agreed. "And Montana?"

"Yeah, boss?"

"Watch your six." I told him.

"Yeah."

"I mean it." I stressed. "I'm not ready to bury another brother, are we clear?"

"Crystal."

Once we were done, I plugged my phone in to charge, grabbed the beer I'd snagged from the kitchen earlier. It had lost some of the coldness since I'd insisted on showering first, but I didn't mind.

The balcony outside my bedroom came in handy. Long after Tianna said she was going to try sleeping, I stood outside, with my beer, trying to put things in the right compartments inside my mind.

I knew what would happen if I tried sleeping.

Sleep wouldn't come and it didn't bother me anymore. I hadn't had a good night's sleep in years.

That's when the demons came—that's when they frolicked and played and turned my world into a dark mass of fear and unease.

The temperature cooled down, and I relish the cold air sliding over my body.

I forced my mind to not go to a place where Tianna existed. Instead, I focused on the work I'd asked Hex to do for me. While she worked on trying to piece together Joseph's movements. I was beginning to formulate others to speak with. Some I'd have to pay, others I'd have to squeeze. I had the money, and I wasn't above laying my hands on those bottom feeders to get what I wanted.

Either way, it had to be done.

I closed my eyes while trying to focus on anything other than the fact Tianna was sleeping down the hall. I tried not thinking of the sheets tangled around her body, a flawless brown thigh sticking out from beneath the blankets.

I took a long drink from my beer and walked over to where I had the phone plugged him. It was late, and usually, Echo would be at *Crosshairs*, working the bar. I took a cleansing breathing and lifted the phone to my ear. "Yeah?" I groaned.

"Sometimes I think you don't love me." Echo teased.

"Aww, but darling, I do better with actions."

Echo laughed.

"Calling to check on me?" I asked, lifting my beer again to my lips for a sip.

"You wound me, sir." Echo giggled. "But yes. I wanted to hear your thoughts on the gorgeous Tianna."

"What do you mean?"

"Come on, Hermes." Echo sighed. "You do realize she's a woman, right?"

"A woman I'm trying to help." I replied. "Sticking my cock into the mix of things can only end badly. I don't want to go there again."

"You know not every woman you meet will be Avery, right?"

I frowned. "She's Montana's ex. They broke up because—" I glanced over my shoulder to ensure I was alone. "She cheated."

Echo sighed. "Yeah, but has she learned from that mistake?"

I shrugged needlessly. "I don't know. And I really don't want to be the tool she uses to find out."

"Okay." Echo's voice restrained. "So, what's your plan? To wander the world aimlessly alone?"

"I'm not alone. I have you."

"I'm not your type. You need a certain kind of woman that I can't be for you."

"And what kind of woman would that be?" I asked. I didn't want to know. But whether I asked her or not, Echo was annoyed, and she was going to let me know precisely what was on her mind.

It was one of the things I loved and hated about her.

"For starters," she said. "When you go home after the world's been shit to you, I can't warm your bed at nights. I can't be the one to hold you during certain things."

I scoffed. "Sex is—"

"You can get sex anywhere you want." She interrupted. "All you have to do is put an ad online and within seconds you have more takers than you care for. The world is a dark, cesspool of sex. Please tell me you realize that this talk is about more than sex."

"Look, Echo—I have to go."

She grunted and hung up.

I drank the rest of my beer, trying to push down the exhaustion and the frustration tear-assing through me.

A soft knock sounded behind me before the door creaked open. Though I felt her with me, I didn't turn to watch her enter.

"Maksim?"

She said my name softly. I trembled.

I'm not strong enough for this.

"There you are." She cheered.

I glanced at her over a shoulder then faced the view again. "I couldn't sleep."

"I'm sorry."

"For what?"

"My family seem to be a hurricane." Tianna stood beside me, the wind blowing her hair.

When I glanced down, I realized she was wearing the shirt I'd given her the first time she spent at my place. She didn't have to anymore. I'd ordered enough clothes for her to have other things to wear. I licked my lips and looked away.

"Well, you and Joseph really don't have to take the credit for this mess." I tried for a joke. "I haven't slept well in a long time. Usually, I spend most of the night tossing and turning."

"You're saying this mess has nothing to do with your insomnia?"

"Not really. I mean, I'm worried about my boys…"

She sighed. "I keep thinking I should walk away."

"And what do you do when they come for you again?"

"I'm trying to do the right thing here!" Tianna pushed at my arm. "I'm trying to walk away from this without anyone else getting hurt. Me leaving will help."

"And if they go after Montana and the others anyway?" He asked.

"I got nothing."

"They had every intention of going after the Protectors." I pulled her into my chest and wrapped my arms around her hips. "We're going to figure this out. We just have to wait while Hex works. In the meantime, I've put Montana on alert. He needs to vet his team."

"Vet them, why?"

"I think one of them sold that information to whoever Joseph got the chip from." I admitted. "If that's the case, someone on the inside his betraying that team and we can't let that be."

Stepping back, she lifted her eyes to mine, her face so close, her breath bathed my cheeks and nose.

"We should get you back to bed." I told her. "The morning comes quickly when you don't want it to."

"In high school, I used to read a lot of romance novels." Her voice husky.

She inched closer.

"I never thought you could be real." Tianna continued.

"Trust me, Anna." I once again tried gathering myself enough, to be a good man and step away from the softness of her body. "I'm no romance hero."

A smile traced her lips as they seemed to be moving closer to mine. I swallowed the lump in my throat and though I knew this shouldn't happen, I remained in place. As the heat of her breath singed my skin hotter and hotter, I closed my eyes and dropped my head the mere inches it took to press my mouth to hers.

Tianna didn't hesitate. She spread her lips for me, and I growled while kissing her as if it would be the last time. Every part of my body came alive and burned with a fire that scared me. But I couldn't stop once our tongues tongued, once a spark of electricity soared through me like ripples on a pond. Her arms tightened around me, bringing me into her.

I wanted to be engulfed by her, to be completely consumed. Even as my hands travelled up her back, one stopping at her neck, the other drifting downward to her ass, I knew this shouldn't keep going. But a swirl of her tongue silenced that annoying voice of denial and I allowed myself to fall into her.

Before I knew it, I had her against the wall, one hand by her head, the other pushing her ass up so her lower half was flush against me, feeling how hard she'd made me.

"Still think I'm a romance hero, Anna?" My voice sounded rough to my ears. "If you knew the things I'm thinking of doing to you right now, you'd realize I'm anything but a good guy."

I tugged at the shirt she wore, clasping her thighs in both hands and reaching for her mouth with mine again. My fingers sank into her supple thighs, and I wanted to howl.

There were very few things sexier than feeling the heat of a woman's thighs, to know how they would feel against the sides of your head.

"Bad girl." I whispered when I slipped one hand between her thigh to find she wasn't wearing panties.

My heart did a strange flip and the hardness in the front of my pants fought to be freed. Knowing she was bare—thinking it was for me, did something to my body. Staring into her eyes, I slipped to my knees in front of her, pushed her shirt up and licked my lips.

Tianna kept herself partially shaved—a landing strip for emphasis, I thought. The view up, between her breasts to the fire in her eyes, propelled me to lean forward. I caught her with my tongue, tasting her hot and sweet.

"Maksim…" She twitched, her body then writhing upward.

Her fingers found my hair.

I reached behind and grabbed her ass, loving the way her cheeks filled my palms. Massaging, squeezing and pushing her forward, I drove her higher, loving her soft sounds, her taste and the way she tugged on my hair.

Tianna came like a storm.

Her thighs shaking in my palms, her clit pulsing on my tongue and her happiness dripping down my chin made me soar. She shouted my name in a way that threatened to upend my world in all the wonderful ways. After kissing the insides of her thighs, I eased upward and bowed my head to kiss her shoulder.

"More." She whispered in my ear before nipping the lob.

Scooping her into my arms, I kissed her while carrying her into my bedroom. After setting her on the bed, she scooted to her butt, hung her legs over the side and kissed my abs. I gasped softly, tossing my head back as her tongue trailed each carved bit of flesh.

I looked down at her and she winked.

Tianna was burning my carnal world to the ground and she had the nerve to wink at me. A low rumble escaped my core as she tugged my trackpants down. I watched her, curious as to if she'd truly go through with it. But soon enough, my toes curled, my eyes rolled back, and I was hers.

I took her in ways I had dreamed about since the moment I saw her. Spreading her wide, getting my fill and giving her everything I had in me.

Each time she came, she dragged her nails down my back, then into my thighs. Tianna was wild—primal, biting my neck, my shoulders, my nipples.

I twisted her in the ways I desired, listened to her cries of passion only to let her fall, catching her on the way down, and doing it all over again.

"Maksim?"

"Yes, baby?" I licked at her neck as I pulled from her and turned her to face the wooden headboards.

She mewled in response and I entered her again.

Tianna tossed her head back and I slipped a palm around her, up over her breasts and to the soft, pulse of her throat. Leaning forward, I kissed her ear, down to her neck, then the spot behind her ears. She came again and slumped forward against the headboard.

Still, I rolled my hips into her, seeking my end, willingly courting my end.

A loud clunk filled the space around me, but I paid it no mind.

Nothing else mattered except her and I—nothing else but the moment we were in.

Nothing.

My orgasm twisted my frame in unexpected ways. It left me shaking while my entire being floated above me. Weak and covered in sweat, I tumbled to the bed which crumbled to the floor beneath the sudden shift of my weight.

Tianna laughed but rested against my chest. "This is your house, right?"

"Yes. Why?" I kissed her head.

"We broke the bed." She pulled the sheets up to her chest and sat up to look down into my face.

She'd been right. My head was now lower than the rest of my body, but I didn't have enough strength to really do anything about it.

Tianna Sharp was beautiful.

Her hair was a mess, her dark skin covered in a light sheen of perspiration, her shoulders bare shoulders begging to be kissed—she was beautiful.

I closed my eyes.

"Please don't regret what we've done." Her voice wavered.

For a moment, I didn't move. It took me a little time to try working out what I heard in her voice. When I looked up at her, she turned away and tried scrambling out of the bed with the sheets still wrapped around her. One end was under my body and she went tumbling to the floor. I rolled to the edge of the bed and it shifted under me, the rest of it clunking to the floor.

I laughed. "You okay?"

"Nothing bruised but my ass and my ego." She scoffed then sighed. "I'm fine."

"One of those things I can kiss better."

She hissed at me.

I smiled down at her but didn't move to help her up. "Look, Anna...I don't regret it."

She stared at me.

"Okay?" I pushed.

Tianna nodded. "You should probably sleep in my room tonight."

I winked at her.

I DIDN'T ASK how a man like Maksim Demidov knew a place like this. It was where the bottom feeders and the idiots went to dwell. It was the darkened bottom of the barrel, the dregs of society. I drew closer to his side, trying to walk straight but also trying not to let every little movement in the corner of my eyes freak me out.

The heavy door clanged close behind me and I gripped his hand.

"Stay close." Hermes told me. "Let me do the talking."

I had no problems with that. Even though the space was anything but full, I didn't want to take any chances.

But Hermes entered the spot in a way that turned me on. He walked with a poise and power, I couldn't help being attracted to. I used that to take my mind off the stench of stale beer and body odor swirling around my head.

Eventually, he stopped.

The man in the seat half buried under partially nude female bodies, looked up and I saw the moment the fear of God entered him. He shoved the women away and surged to his feet. I knew he was trying to run but he didn't get far. Hermes grabbed him by the back of the neck and slammed him into the leather booth.

The girls stared at Hermes who gave them as much attention as a fly about to be crushed under his foot. One girl exhaled and Hermes shifted to glare at her.

"Shoo!" He said.

They scrambled away from the table and Hermes sat.

I didn't. My body couldn't seem to hear a thing my brain was saying except for *panic.*

Hermes took my hand and gently tugged me into the chair beside him then leaned in to speak to the terrified man on the other side.

"I've stayed off your radar, Hermes." The man stammered. "Why are you here?"

"Joseph Sharp." Hermes replied. "Speak."

"Come on, man. He's nothing but trouble." The man replied. "What do you want to know about him? Asking around can get your wings clipped—you know that, right? He's dead. Leave it alone."

His words hit a little close to home but before I could say anything, Hermes reached cross, grabbed him by the neck and slammed him face first into the table. When he yelped and jerked back, blood trickled from his nose.

I gripped his thigh under the table, but he didn't so much as look my way. Glancing around the room, I could tell the others saw what happened, but none of them moved to help the terrified man. Hermes leaned back in the seat and lowered his angry gaze on his prey.

"You know better." Hermes growled at him.

"Look, I don't want any trouble." The man stuttered, using a napkin to blot at his nose. "I just want to sit here with my bitches and have a drink. You walk in here, asking about Joseph Sharp is just not okay or safe."

"You know how I get when I have to repeat myself." Hermes growled.

"I know Joseph is dead." The man spoke, leaning forward. "He was greedy. Nothing was ever good enough for him—even enough wasn't good enough. I warned him, to take the money and walk away."

"Why walk away?" Hermes asked.

"Because how lucky can one person be?" The man asked. "The luck only holds out so long. Shit, after a while even the adrenaline doesn't feel the same. But he said he had one final score to settle. He asked me if I wanted in, but I took my share of the money and bounced. I know when my luck is done."

"What money?" Hermes asked.

"We did a score in Pickering two months ago—walked out with two and a half mil large. I told Joseph it was my last. We both got out with a little over one million." He picked up his glass, realized it was empty and frowned. He dropped the glass on the table. "But Joseph had always had more balls than brains. Somewhere along the way he came across this chip—I had no idea what was on it or even where he got it from. He tried cutting me in, but something was off."

"Like what." I asked.

He glanced at me.

"Answer the lady." Hermes told him slowly.

"For one, I was enjoying my money—investing, you know? I was done with the life." He replied, his eyes dipping to my breasts until Rei slapped his cheek. He cleared his throat and returned his gaze to Rei. "Secondly, he was way too excited about it. Anyway, he calls up Massimo Slova."

"Slova?" Hermes asked. "The ex Green Beret?"

The man nodded.

"You're lying." Hermes snapped. "Slova is dead."

"You should know better, Hermes. Just because the military tell you someone is dead, doesn't mean they are." The man spat.

Hermes grunted.

"Look." The man wiped the rest of the blood from his nose into his sleeve then looked up. "The bottom line is, Joseph stole something that was meant to go to Slova, he found out and now Joseph is dead. Someone has to pay the piper."

"Let's say I believe you." Hermes began. "What's Slova doing this side of the border? His vice is guns. Canada isn't where the money is for that."

"It's not about the money." The man reached for the bottle of tequila at the corner of the table. "Someone tried to kill him, apparently, Slova thought it was Joe."

"Please—Joe's motive is to hit 'em hard, take what he can and running." I pointed out.

"Yeah? Tell that to Slova." The man muttered. "He wants someone to pay for it. Joseph dying already was an accident. They don't know where the key is. You're his sister, aren't you?"

I nodded.

"They coming for you?"

"Yeah."

The man scoffed. "If Slova wants someone dead— no use running."

"He'll get to her over my dead body." Hermes' voice was dark.

But the man across from him didn't so much as flinch. "I don't think I have to tell you that they can arrange that."

"Where do I find Slova?" Hermes asked.

"Come on, Hermes." He whined. "I've already told you too much."

"Obviously not enough because I still have questions." Hermes warned.

The man sighed. "The thing is, it's harder for him because Joseph is dead, and the chip is missing."

"Not a very smart criminal." I broke the rules. "You get the goods before you kill the man. Isn't that how it's supposed to work?"

"I don't know what to tell you." The man replied. "Death was never my thing. I borrow without permission but never with weapons. I'm greedy not stupid. But like I told you before, it was an accident, Joseph getting killed. He sent morons to do the job instead of going himself—his first mistake."

"Trust me." Hermes exhaled. "That wasn't his first mistake."

Hermes glanced over his shoulder just as his phone rang. He held up a finger to answer it then frowned and dumped the cell into his pocket.

"You should get out of here." Hermes told the canary. "We're about to have company."

The man scrambled from the booth and disappeared through a dark curtain the back. Hermes rose and pulled a gun from the back of his pants. He did something to it then handed it to me.

"Point and fire." He told me.

"Hermes…"

"No. If something happens to me, you point and you fire." He stressed. "Got it."

"Got it."

The front door exploded and some very pissed off men stepped through. The shock of it sent the gun he'd given me skittering across the floor and I swore.

"Leave it for now." Hermes barked. "I need you to pay attention."

The room didn't have much place to hide and soon they made a beeline for us. Hermes grabbed my hand but eased his large frame a little in front of me.

When the world erupted into fighting around me, my first instinct was to hide. But seeing Hermes cutting through the men like they were simply drywall, pushed something through me that had me cracking a chair over the head of one of the men. I put all my body into the swing and watched him slumped to the floor.

He wasn't unconscious.

I kicked him in the ribs until he merely curled in on himself.

Someone grabbed me around the waist, and I reached for the open bottle of whiskey on a nearby table and jabbed it backward.

The person screamed and released me, shoving me forward. I stopped myself from falling by bracing my palms on the table, picked up a glass and swirled on the man now rubbing his eyes. I missed as he staggered back, but I didn't let up. I stepped forward, bringing my knee up into his dick.

"Fuck!" He seemed to forget about the pain in his eyes and grabbed himself.

"You're welcome!" I spat.

"Anna!" Hermes called.

The warning didn't come fast enough. Someone hit me so hard in the back, it felt as though my spine wanted to peel itself out my chest. I went flying across the room and stopped against the glass bottles behind the bar.

When I hit the ground, I was showered in liquid and glass. Covering my head and face with my arms, I screamed and curled into a ball to protect myself. Glass sliced through my arms, my shoulder and side. When it stopped, the alcohol rain was a mere pitter-patter, I groaned at the pain to tear through me.

"Anna?" Hermes called before strong arms gripped my shoulders. "Baby?"

I groaned and tried looking up but was afraid alcohol would fill my eyes. "Hmm?"

"Are you hurt?"

"A little, but I'm okay."

He helped me to my feet and was leading me somewhere. The cool air of the outside rushed over my face and he stopped to clean my face with large fingers.

"Come on." Hermes took my hand and led me back to the vehicle.

He peeled away from the location and sped off down the road while I tried picking pieces of glass from my hair, my arm while my entire body burned.

Hermes called Hex and told her to find all she could on Slova. Hex hadn't been pleased to hear that name. It seemed the man was a piece of work.

"Why are you asking about him?" Hex asked. "He's dead—let him rest in chaos."

"Well, he just sent men to kill Anna and I." Hermes told her. "The last time I checked, ghosts don't do that. And if he's a fucking ghost, I want him gone. Do as I ask, please."

"What? Are you sure?" Hex asked.

"According to Frog, that's what that was." Hermes told her. "Find him, Hex."

"Was Frog sober?" Hex asked. "I mean the man hasn't out down a bottle since he was discharged."

"Hex."

I knew the sound of Hermes losing what tenuous hold he had left on his temper and it was that one word.

"On it." She said.

He leaned forward and disconnected the call but didn't look at me. All he did was press his foot down on the gas a little harder.

"What do you know about this Slova guy?" I asked.

"He was Green Beret." Hermes checked the mirrors then swung out of the lane he was in to run through a traffic light on yellow. "Then figured there was more money in contracting. He began getting paid by the military to do construction work for them abroad. But his greed has led him down the road of selling his services to the highest bidder."

"So, he's a mercenary."

"Kind of." He replied. "He's been accused of bringing things into the country he shouldn't…"

"Guns, drugs…prostitutes."

Hermes headed left on Adelaide then pulled onto Queen Street and headed east.

"Why does he want the information on Montana and his guys?"

"Because Montana was responsible for taking him down the first time." Hermes admitted. "But the mission didn't go as it was supposed to. This guy tried using a child as a human shield."

I gasped.

"Long story short is, he's supposed to be dead." Hermes glanced over his shoulder.

"So, what you're telling me is that this is about revenge?" I wanted to know.

"Seems that way." Hermes replied. "We're going to get you cleaned up, then we have a conference with Hex. Kujo is on his way here to give us a hand and depends on how things are, we'll try getting Echo to help us out."

"I don't want to bring all these people into my hell."

I chuckled. "You wanna tell Echo her friends were in danger and we didn't tell her? She'd kick my ass for not knowing better and strangle you for keeping me from telling her."

"Dang." I laughed softly at his joke even though my whole body was one big ache. "Only if we need them, okay?"

"Deal. But Kujo is already inbound."

I wanted to curl into Hermes' arms and stay there. As he'd held me all night, I couldn't remember feeling so protected, so safe. They said there was no such thing as perfection.

The person who came up with that quote most not have had a Hermes.

Being cuddled into him was the most perfect thing in the world—and I'd had a chance to experience that.

Soon, I'd be one my way back home or dead—either way, that meant no more Hermes.

And that made me overwhelmingly sad.

Later, Hermes cleaned my wounds as gently as he could. He placed a band-aid just over my left eyebrow, then helped me with checking the rest of my body for any sliver of glass that may have sliced through me. There weren't any surprises and after a shot of whiskey, he pulled me into his arms on the sofa.

I didn't complain. I snuggled into his side and rested my head on his chest, listening to the calm way his heartbeat as in some special rhythm to life. He kissed my head, and I buried my face into his neck trying to stop the way my eyes burned with unshed tears.

"I'm sorry I'm a shit human being." I told him when I was finally strong enough to merely settled on him again. "This is all my fault."

"How?" He asked.

"If I hadn't been such a dog to Montana…"

"Anna, that's not how the world works." Hermes told me. "I mean, if that was how the world works, I'd be screwed. I've done some horrible things in the name of patriotism and country."

"It's not the same." I muttered. "The punishment for breaking someone's heart his worse. Karma doesn't like that."

"You really don't believe that, do you?" Hermes asked. "These things happen. I'm not a fan of it, but people cheat—all the time. The divorce rate because of cheating is astronomical. But not everyone has their lives torn apart because their brother is a dick."

I sighed and sat up. "I'm sorry—I figure I should say that now before—"

"No." Hermes snapped. "Stop it right now. We know who's behind this. All we have to do is hear all the details then come up with a plan."

I framed the right side of his face with my palm and stared into his eyes. I saw now why Montana had sent me to him. Maksim Demidov may look like a jock, and he may be sexy as hell, but at his core he was a good man.

He was special.

"Maksim?" I whispered, my heart floating inside my chest.

"Hmm?" He rested his head back to the sofa and kept me captive with his gaze.

"Maksim…"

"Don't be afraid to say what's on your mind."

"It's what I want." I managed, swallowing the lump in my throat. "I don't—I mean, I shouldn't."

Hermes lifted his head to stare at me. "Show me."

Exhaling loudly, I climbed into his lap and kissed him as deeply as I could. By the time his large palms grabbed my ass cheeks, I was all about him. He stripped me on the sofa, careful of my bruises and scrapes. I spread myself for him right there in the living room.

Except this time, he was gentle, so tender I couldn't stop the tears from streaming down my face as he licked down my frame. He stopped to kiss my hips, the soft insides of my thighs then lower.

I arched upward, ignoring the burning of my wounds to bury my fingers in his hair and move his tongue where I truly wanted it.

The first time my world shattered for him, I bit into a knuckle to stop the sound.

The second time, I had no control. My eyes snapped opened as I whispered his name the screamed out loud. My frame trembled but he didn't give me time to breath. He took me hard and deep and my entire world vanished. All the darkness I had been feeling the past few days had been illuminated by a beautiful light only Hermes could shine into my soul.

In return, I did everything I could to hear him growl for me again. I did everything to feel him surging inside me like the waves of the ocean during a storm—rough and powerful.

How was I going to let this go?

How was I going to stop thinking about the warmth of his frame, the strength in his touch—all of it?

A roll of his hips took my mind back to a place where all I could think about was him.

"Maksim…"

"Come for me." He whispered against my ear. "Forget everything else. For the next little while, I'm yours. All of me—every bit of me."

I came again—so hard, I thought my heart must have stopped for a split second.

I didn't care.

"You're mine." I panted, dragging my nails down his back to sink them into the meaty flesh of his ass. "You're mine."

MAKSIM DEMIDOV

THE RAIN CAME unannounced and the temperature dropped. It wasn't cold enough for heaters, but I had to dig out a couple blankets for Tianna. While she stayed with Kujo, I left the house we were staying at, to pay someone a visit. I had Hex track my phone, just in case.

The massage parlor stood in the center of the city, a prestigious neighborhood. The neighbors didn't complain because for the most part, it's a quiet place, closed at the end of business hours and the clients who went in pulled up in expensive cars and three-piece suits.

On the inside of *The Compound Nail and Spa Services,* everything was all but legit. I rolled the Maserati into a slot and slipped on my designer sunglasses. When I stepped from the car, I noticed the curtain from a home across the way slipped back in place.

I turned and headed up the front steps and into the comfortable interior of the Spa. A petite woman at the front desk greeted me with a smile.

"How may we assist you today?" She asked.

"I'm Maksim Demidov." I told her.

"Wow." Her eyes widened. "The billionaire... welcome to our spa!"

"Thank you. I'm actually here looking for services for my girlfriend." I lied easily while picking up a pamphlet.

"Girlfriend?" She sputtered. "I didn't—I mean, okay."

"She's been working very hard lately. I wanted her to have a day of pampering. Money is no problem. I want her to have the best."

I took in where the cameras were while pretending to read the pamphlet.

"She's a lucky woman."

I smiled.

"Oh, I assure you our services are tops in the city." She replied excitedly. "The first thing we do, is give you a tour of the premises—the parts that do not violate our clients' privacy, of course."

"Of course."

"If I could have you fill this out." She collected a form with a clipboard then directed me to the seating area. "I will have someone come out to give you the tour presently. It'll be easier to pick the services if you can see a few of them."

I nodded.

To their credit, they had a young woman exit to show me around. She babbled excitedly about the different places in the spa, the different services, which was her favorite. When she left to gather more paperwork, I found the room I wanted, entered and closed the door behind me. I stood behind the man with the towel over his face and frowned while I turned up the heat keeping the heated rocks warm.

"I didn't think you were coming back, Sweetie." He spoke without moving. "Daddy's been aching for a release."

I gripped the ends of the towel on both sides and pulled it down tightly over his face, keeping his head into the headrest while he struggled.

"If you keep struggling you will break your neck." I growled close to his ear. "Usually, I wouldn't mind. But I need some information from you first before that happens."

"Who are you?"

"I think you've forgotten how this works." I cranked the towel down even tighter. "Let me remind you. I ask the questions. You answer them. Truthfully."

"I ain't telling you shit!"

"And you're sure that's the stance you want to take?" I asked. "I mean, I'm a good guy—I was going to walk away once I find out what I need. But now? Well, now I'm just going to have to fuck you up."

"What do you mean by that?" He stopped struggling for a second. "No, I'm not telling you anything."

"Too bad." I set a palm over his face to keep him in place then reached for the large tong to pick up one of the hot rocks. Without a second thought, set it on his chest.

The stone had gotten hotter than they were supposed to. The moment it hit his skin the air erupted in hissing and a stench of burnt flesh.

To think, it used to bother me.

When he screamed, I covered the part of the towel where his mouth was to kill his sound. With my free hand, I picked up another rock and set it on his junk. He twisted against my hold, but I merely settled him with a hand on his forehead.

"You don't have to talk, Kevin." I told him. "But I'm not just going to leave without having a little fun. Now, where do I put the next rock?"

Kevin tried to speak but my hand was still over his mouth.

I lifted it. "I'm sorry. What was that?"

"You son of a bitch!"

I picked up another rock and placed it on one thigh.

It hissed.

"What do you want?" He grunted.

"That's better." I relaxed my hold. "Tell me what Solva wants with the Brotherhood Protectors."

"I don't know what you're talking about."

"I still have tons of rocks left, Kevin. I don't like it when you lie to me."

"Solva is holding a grudge." Kevin sputtered. "He said they tried to kill him."

"Why is he in Canada if he wants revenge on the Protectors?"

"He hid here after he faked his own death." Kevin explained. "He's only biding his time before he goes back. But his plans were screwed up when someone stole the information, he was waiting on to use against the BP. He tried getting it back, but the guy accidentally got killed."

"Who gave him info on the BP?"

"That's the secret." Kevin grunted. "No one seem to know where he got all that information from but..."

"Guess."

"I'm not saying. You'll just hurt me more."

"I'll hurt you more if you don't tell me. So, what do you have to lose?"

Kevin sobbed. "I guess it's someone on the inside —I know how you military types are. All about loyalty and shit—but sometimes loyalties can be bought and Solva is stinking rich."

"Where is Solva?" I asked.

"He has a house in Pickering, but he doesn't really live there." Kevin told me. "He's always afraid someone is coming after him, so he's constantly moving around. Now, I've told you all I know! I need a doctor."

But I couldn't let him know who I was. He could squeal to Solva, then I'd lose the element of surprise and someone I cared about would get hurt—Tianna could get hurt.

After knocking Kevin unconscious, I ensured his face was covered again and slipped out the door on the other side of the room. It led me along a corridor that let me out a door that said it was an emergency exit.

It wasn't on an alarm. I assumed it was a side door for certain clients to sneak in and for them to get out of the place happened to be raided.

By the time I was making it back home, the anger I felt for Solva threatened to take over my entire soul. This was a man who was using American military contracts to run drugs, guns and God knows what else into the country. He swore to protect our people, leave no man behind and a whole slew of other rules we automatically adhere to when we signed up to be soldiers.

They brought things into the country to kill our people in ways I didn't even want to think about.

They lied and cheated and killed two of their own.

Now, this asshole was after Tianna—I smirked.

Time to make him pay.

Making it back to the place we were staying, was easy enough. Tianna was asleep on the sofa, a blanket pulled up to her shoulders while Kujo made a sandwich in the kitchen. I flopped on one of the stools and Kujo looked.

"Did you find what you were looking for?" Kujo asked.

"Unfortunately." I muttered, then proceeded to tell him everything. "This man is responsible for ruining so many lives. How in the hell did you guys miss?"

Kujo exhaled heavily. "It happens. You should know that."

"They don't know where he is." I explained to Kujo. "He keeps moving."

"I guess when you're an evil asshole there's always cause to keep looking over your shoulder." Kujo hissed. "Listen, man. I'm sorry. Somewhere along the line we fucked up."

"Think it could have been dirty intel?"

"Who knows?" Kujo pushed his sandwiched away from in front of him. "But back then everything was such a rush. We went in blind, barely any knowledge of the layout of the land. And they were sending us in to take down one of our own."

I sighed. "She's in danger, Kujo. Her sorry excuse of a brother brought her into this and there doesn't seem to be anything I can do but sit on my hands while spinning in fucking circles."

"The first thing you're going to do, is calm down." Kujo told me. "Then, you're going to put Hex and Swede together. We're going to find this son of a bitch and we're going to kick his ass. Got it?"

I said nothing. This time when we pull the trigger, if it came to that, I'd make sure he was double tapped to the chest.

This time, that son-of-a-bitch was going down —hard.

Instead of speaking out loud, I pulled out my cell and made a video call to Hex.

"You're on speaker." I warned her. "Behave yourself."

"It doesn't matter, darling." She teased, her voice dipping low. "When it comes to you, I like being watched."

Kujo laughed. "Hello, Hexadecimal."

She smirked. "Hi Kujo. How's Six?"

"Still the best doggo on the planet." Kujo laughed.

"I'm due for some Six cuddles but in the meantime, let's get down to business." She paused to type away at her keyboard. "Hermes, I need you to be on the big screen for this."

Kujo and I exchanged looks but we wandered down to my office. Hex hacked herself into the system and her face slid to the right top side of the screen. Her screen appeared on mine so we could watch surveillance.

"So," Hex said. "Joseph had been a very busy boy the days leading up to his death. "He spent most of his time at that hotel, but other than that, he has this bar in Burlington where I found him a few nights. The night before two days before he went poof into thin air, he was at the Carlyle."

"What was he doing there?" I asked.

"What's the Carlyle?" Kujo asked.

"It's an underground bar." I replied thoughtfully.

"Underground—as in speakeasy or a place where a man like Solva would go to without fear of being caught?"

"Speakeasy? Not so much. A man like Solva can go there without fear he'll be caught..." Hex reported.

"Son of a bitch..." I muttered.

Silence.

"I think you should pull his string." Hex joked. "I think we broke him."

"No—this makes sense." I told them. "First, we're going to need to gather some intel."

"You or I can't just walk in there and have a look around." Kujo pointed out. "He knows our faces. Tianna nor Hex can't either."

"I have a friend." I told them. "Hex, you think Knight would be up to doing us a favor?"

Hex smirked. "You know that man, always walking on the wild side. Why don't you ask?"

I agreed and she continued going through the information she's found on Solva. There wasn't much but she was able to dig up a bunch of aliases that he'd been using. There wasn't a surprise about where his money was coming from. It was all from illegal dealings.

What was surprising, however, was that so many people could have been bought to allow him to do whatever he wanted.

I rubbed my eyes then put in a call to Slade Titan.

"The trickster God." Knight answered his phone. "How's it?"

I laughed. "I've been better." I replied. "Listen, I was calling for a little help. You think you might be in?"

"What kind of help?"

"A friend of mine is in trouble." I replied. "We found out who is after her, but we need intel before we take the fool down."

"He knows what you guys look like." It was more of a statement than a question on Knight's part.

I chuckled. "Precisely."

"I'm in—especially if your *friend* is a pretty one."

His words caused me to choke on air. "She is."

"And yours, I take it."

"Um—I'm not sure yet."

"But you want." Knight pushed.

He'd always had this uncanny way of reading me. "Something like that."

"Well, let me get some things finished here, have someone cover me then I'll call you to figure out where you are." Knight told me. "I'm going to need more info."

"For sure."

I hung up and exhaled loudly. Kujo and I wandered out of the office, but Tianna was still sleeping. Seeing her there, peaceful, her nose flaring as she snored softly made me smile. She'd kicked the blanket off and I pulled it back up to her shoulders, pushed a strand of hair back and behind her ear and remained there, watching her face.

Though I knew Kujo was watching me, I couldn't seem to help myself. I knew she wouldn't want him to know we'd been intimate. Kujo was Montana's friend—they loved each other and probably had no secrets from each other.

It wouldn't be fair to ask Kujo to keep one now.

I rose and walked with him through the kitchen, stopping only to grab a beer then out the back door unto the patio. Neither of us spoke until after we'd wrung the caps from our drinks and had taken a few healthy sips.

"You do know what you're doing, right?" Kujo asked.

"No clue."

"Okay." Kujo spoke softly. "You do know her and Montana…"

"I know." I replied around another big gulp of booze. "I know and I get I'm breaking one of those unwritten rules of the manhood brotherhood, but—"

"That's the dumbest thing I've ever heard." Kujo shook his head. "Look, when the two of them dated, they were both young. Neither of them was prepared for what a serious relationship should have been or should have meant. Montana took it too seriously. Tianna didn't take it serious enough."

"I'd say. She slept with someone else."

"Right." Kujo lifted his drink to his lips, hesitated then lowered it without a taste. "I'm pretty sure Montana doesn't have a say in who she moves on with. He's married and happy. If Tianna makes you happy, then go for it."

"I feel as if I'm betraying Montana."

"You're not." Kujo assured me. "When you break up with someone you don't have claim over them anymore. And I think he'd be the first person to tell you all that. We can't help who we're attracted to. Plus, I'm sure I don't have to tell you that Tianna Sharp is a good-looking woman."

My cheeks threatened to burn me alive. To cool my body down, I drank deeply from my bottle. "You don't have to tell me. I've seen parts of that woman I'm sure even Montana hasn't seen."

"Damn."

I chuckled. "All I'm saying, is there is something there. It's not love—not yet."

"Let me ask you this." Kujo shifted to look at me after glancing over his shoulders. "Can you see yourself falling in love with her?"

The answer threatened to erupt out my lips. But as an adult, once certain words were in the universe, there was nothing that could be done to take them back. I lifted my bottle to my lips, using the time between pulling some of the cold, slightly bitter liquid into my mouth and swallowing, to gather my thoughts. "Yes." I finally replied. "I can see myself falling in love with her. What she did to Montana was horrible, but I'd like to think she's grown up since then. Then again, this could be just a waste of emotions."

"Why is that?"

"She'll be going home at the end of this."

"And?" Kujo asked.

"Long distance?"

"Hermes—brother—you have more money than a good ninety eight percent of this country. Hell, you have more money than most of the people on this damn planet. Use some of it to make yourself happy."

I sighed.

"Now—what did Knight say?"

"He has to finish some things then he'd call me back." I drained the bottle. "But he's in."

Kujo nodded. "I'm going to stretch my back out a

little bit and call my girl. It won't be a short conversation."

"Um—what?"

"Maybe you should see if Tianna wants something to—er—eat."

I tilted my head.

Kujo winked at me and entered the house again. I shook my head but couldn't help smiling at the suggestion. The idea of getting a taste of her in that moment wasn't a bad thing—it didn't turn me off. In fact, my heart raced inside my chest.

I dropped my beer bottle in the recycle bin, then made my way into the living room. Tianna was now on her back, the blanket down to her hips. Her shirt had shifted, exposing more of one breast. I brushed it with a knuckle, and she moaned. She didn't wake up, even after I tugged the blanket from her body, knelt at her feet and spread her legs.

Tianna moaned my name.

My tongue found her wet and ready. I wasn't sure what her dream was about, but I was certain it was a hot one. I sucked on her clit, feeling it pulse gently on my tongue as she dripped down my chin. She whispered my name, her fingers found my hair and I lifted my head to see she was awake.

"Maksim, Kujo is here." She panted but was already pushing my head back between her luscious thighs.

"He's taking a nap." I told her. "The only way he'll hear is if you scream."

"I won't scream."

"Challenge accepted!"

"Hermes that wasn't a—"

I curled my tongue around her clit then sucked it into my mouth.

"Mmm! Don't stop!"

I WISHED we had eyes in the club. The fact Knight was going in alone bothered me. He was a stranger to me, someone who shouldn't have had to do any of this. But again, my brother was an idiot, and this was what my life had come to.

I wanted Knight to have backup—just in case of anything. But Hermes, Knight and Kujo all agreed it was better not to have anything suspicious on him. Knight felt it would be easy enough for a trained eye to recognize a hidden camera.

Not knowing what was happening drove me crazy. I paced the living room until Kujo helped me into one of the seats.

But that didn't last.

Hermes excused himself to tackle a business call. I realized then for all the wealth I saw around him, I wasn't really sure what he did for his month. It also dawned on me I was once again left alone with one of Montana's friends. The first time, I pretended to be asleep until I truly fell asleep. This time, I was too buzzed to actually sleep.

"What?" I asked when his eyes followed me one way then the next.

"I don't trust you." Kujo spoke honestly.

"What?"

"With Hermes." He explained. "I don't trust you."

"What are you talking about?" I demanded.

"Really?" Kujo scoffed. "Come on. Only a blind man wouldn't see the way you look at him."

"He's also a grown man!" I reminded him. "I'm sure he doesn't need you to protect him."

"Then who will?"

Silence.

It was the kind of quiet I was pretty sure happened before the world ended.

"This is ridiculous!" I snapped. "It was a lifetime ago."

Kujo cleared his throat. "I'm sorry, what?"

"Don't what me." I told him. "I heard what you just said. Plus, I've seen the way you look at me. Yes, Montana and I dated. Yes, I was an idiot, but there is only so many times I can apologise before it starts meaning nothing."

He sat in the overstuffed chair like a king on a thrown and levelled his gaze on me. "I didn't say anything."

"You didn't have to." I tossed my hands up as I paced one way then the next. "And I like Hermes. I really do. I won't let you ruin this for me."

"I'm not the one you should be worried about ruining this, Tianna." Kujo told me. "My question is this. Have you learned from the past, or is Hermes just another toy for you?'"

My first instinct was to slap him. I wanted to slap him so hard he saw stars. I wanted to slap him until my hands were tired and the world turned from darkness to light. But I sat on my hands and glared at him. "What's that supposed to mean?"

"Whatever you want it to mean."

Kujo's accusations were infuriating.

"You have a record of hurting the people I care about." He pointed out. "I don't want it happening again. I'm sure you get that."

"People? I hurt one person—a gazillion years ago!" I whispered hoarsely. "And yes, I'm quite aware it was wrong. But both he and I have moved on from that. No one seems to be able to let it go except the person I hurt. I've made amends with Montana. He's with someone else and happy. It's not fair to ask me to pay for that one mistake with the rest of my life."

"I'm not asking you to do anything. Like I said before, I don't want history repeating itself." Kujo leaned forward to stare into my eyes. "Hermes is a good man—one of the best friends a guy could ever ask for. I don't want you going into this if you think you're just going to give what's his to someone else."

"Are you calling me a slut?"

Kujo smiled—it was the same kind of slow smile Montana had given me the day he told me not to contact him again unless I was dead or bleeding to death. "If the shoe fits."

The sound to erupt my throat scared even me. But Kujo didn't even flinch. Before I could tell him off, Hermes entered the room again and I pushed my back into the rear of my seat to keep from bolting.

Still, I sketched while the two of them talk. It was the only thing I could do to keep from either crying or murder Kujo.

By the time Knight returned, he walked in with Echo in tow. Apparently, she was his backup and she looked like a model.

"Damn." I mused.

She giggled and did a twirl. "You like?"

"You look good." I told her. "That top looks familiar."

"It should." She wandered into the kitchen. "It's one of yours."

I laughed. "Oh Jesus."

I followed her into the kitchen and took a better look at the top. It was indeed one of my designs when I was working with a design house fresh out of college. It had been a while since I did any of that kind of work.

Now, I freelanced, working for the wealthy and celebrities who wanted one-of-a-kind pieces. I didn't have a store or a team. It was just me, working like a maniac.

The idea of opening my own boutique store flashed in my mind and again, I silenced it with a deep breath.

Echo and I gathered snacks and drinks for everyone and went back to join the guys. Hex was now on the television screen. When we sat, the meeting began.

"Solva is there." Knight reported. "Apparently, it's his haunt. I got a regular drunk and asked him some questions. Turns out, Solva owns a part of the bar. He's a very silent partner. He can be found there almost nightly. The thing is, there are only two ways into the place but it's a maze down there."

Knight borrowed my pencil and ripped a page from my sketchpad to draw.

"Okay, when you go in the front door." He scribbled. "You have to go down about three flights of stairs, along this maddening corridor, through another set of halls until you empty out into what looks like a bomb shelter."

"Why all that?" I asked.

"It's a way to make sure they can't be raided." Echo pointed out.

"They can still get raided." I told her. "The cops just have to get in."

"Yes." Hermes eased forward and pointed to what Knight was still drawing on. "But it makes it harder to be raided. Even unsafe for law enforcement. Between the stairs and the corridor, there has to be cameras, sensors set up…"

"A waring system." I mused.

"That's right." Hermes agreed, pride in his voice. "The room Knight described as a bomb shelter probably have a heavy metal door that can only be locked and opened from one side. Right?"

Knight nodded.

I frowned. "That way if they get breached, all they have to do is have someone lock the door here—" I pointed to the drawing. "And whoever is on the other side can't get in."

"That's right." Echo nodded.

"That also means, there is another way in and out." I told them.

Knight nodded. "The second door I saw has to be it. Or, they have another way somewhere hidden where only those who work there knows about."

"So, how are we going to get in?" I wanted to know. "If we can't get from the entry to here without being seen and we don't know where the secondary door is or empties out?"

"Well." Hermes stared at the rough drawing. "Hex, can you get into their system?"

"That's the beauty about being underground." Hex was typing away, the irritation on her face told me everything. "I can't get a signal on anything. That means, their cameras are just for monitoring, nothing needing any real network."

"They still don't know the real reason we were there." Echo pointed out.

"How did you even get in?" I asked. "It's not like they're letting just anyone in."

"My brother and I are known." Knight replied. "We can pretty much buy our way into any place we'd like. We don't make it a habit but right now it was necessary."

"So, I could be Knight's date." Echo suggested. "That would get us in. Then we could probably figure out a way to get the others in."

"Or—I could try figuring out where the other exit is." Hex cut through the suggestions. "Using the blueprint for the buildings in that geographical area, I should be able to narrow the possibilities down. Afterward, you guys will have to go and confirm."

"How close can you guess?" Kujo questioned.

"Not sure. I've never actually done this before." Hex told us as maps began popping up on the large screen. "That's why I suggested you go and check it out before you commit."

"Hermes?" Echo asked.

"Okay, Kujo, you should get some rest," Hermes said. "Echo, Knight, you guys head home for now. Once Hex gets us the location, Tianna and I will go check it out. Once we have an idea, I'll call you."

"Okay." Knight nodded. "When you do find something, I'll grab Thunder on our way back. The more eyes we can have in this, the better."

Hermes agreed and soon we were alone in his living room. The heat of his stare trailed my skin, and I bit back a shiver. I tried focusing on the art I was working on, but it was hard.

"What's the matter?" Hermes asked.

"You told Kujo about us?"

"Was it supposed to be a secret?" He asked.

"Maybe."

Hermes laughed softly. "I don't want to be a secret, Tianna." He exhaled and when I looked up, he was rubbing his eyes. "Never mind. Okay? I can see where this is going and frankly, I don't have the patience or the energy. I don't want to walk down that road with anyone."

He was out of his chair and out of the room before I could even exhale properly. Dropping my sketchpad and pencil on the sofa and darted after him. I caught him descending the stairs toward his garage. "Wait a minute!" I grabbed his arm, stepped around him and braced my palms to his chest.

"Your friends hate me." I told him. "And I get why. But I can't keep paying for that."

"Are you fucking my friends?" He snapped.

"What? No!"

"Then what's the problem?"

"The problem is, from now on, every time I

meet up with one of them, they'll read me the riot act!" I told him honestly. "They don't want you getting hurt. I get it. But I refuse to keep feeling like dried ass because of something I did over a decade ago."

"Are you going to hurt me?"

"Not on purpose!" I wanted to cry. "Never on purpose."

Hermes' muscular shoulders rose and fell. "I'll have a talk with them, okay?"

"I don't want that either."

"Tianna—you have a history." Hermes pointed out. "They know that. and they worry. That's what friends do. But in all fairness, I'm the one you're sleeping with. And if we decide to take this to the next level, I'm the one you should be focused on."

He sighed.

"It's not fair to you to have to deal with their ire." He admitted. "You're right. And if it keeps happening will you let me speak to them about it?"

"Sure." I nodded.

"But I'm going to need you to take some time after all this, to think about what you want from me. Because once we're together, if you give away what's mine, I'll never forgive you."

My heart broke at the pain in his eyes. Cheating on Montana was the worse thing I'd ever done—ever. It caused so much pain—pain I was still suffering from.

Still, I nodded. "I'm going to ask you for the same thing in return."

"What's that?"

"That you don't give away what's mine." I replied, lifting my chin to meet his beautiful eyes. "I know I have no right to ask that."

"Why not?"

"Because of…"

Hermes leaned his back into the wall. "How about this—how about we agree to leave the past there? Isn't it hard to walk with that monkey on your back?"

"I know how Atlas felt."

He framed one side of my face, caressing my cheek with his thumb. "Then let it go. Don't carry Montana into this with me. I love the man, but I don't want him in my bed—understand?"

I nodded.

"Words, Anna."

Instead of speaking, I stepped forward and cuddled myself against his chest. I tucked my head under his chin and held on as tightly as he could.

"Hey." Hermes whispered. "Darling, talk to me."

"I'm sorry I wasn't stronger." My voice cracked. "That I didn't carry myself in a way that wouldn't cause all this—this—confusion."

"I'm not confused, Anna." He told me simply. "I know what I want. But we can discuss that later. Right now, you should probably try getting some rest. Hex should be calling us back any time and you and I will have to go hunting."

I wanted to argue. I wanted to take him back to bed with me. But he was in a mood and I figured he could use some time by himself. The only thing I could do as brace my palms to his chest, pushed to my tiptoes and kiss him.

Hermes held the back of my neck with a large palm to keep my lips against his a little longer then released me. After a deep breath, I made my way back into the living room to find Kujo looking down at something. When I realized what it was, I sighed and snatched it from his hand.

"That's private." I snapped, then stopped to gather my sketchbook.

"It's good." Kujo turned toward the kitchen. "I especially like the knife sticking out of my eye."

"That was my therapy. You shouldn't have seen that."

"Obviously." Kujo replied. "I'm not going to apologize."

"Look, I know you're looking out for Hermes." I hugged the book to my chest and followed. "But I'm not the same person I was when Montana and I ended."

"Everyone changes." He stopped to stare at me, as if reading me. "I hope. Look, Tianna, I don't have anything against you. My knee-jerk reaction when it comes to my brothers is to—"

"Protect them with your life."

"Yes. It's a war thing." He winked at me.

"Honestly?"

Kujo nodded.

"I didn't come here expecting any of this." I explain to him. "As women we have to recognize good men when we see them. And sometimes we screw up. But once we know what that mistake feels like, the smart ones don't want to experience it again."

"And you're one of the smart ones?"

"You damn right." I replied quickly. "This may not work out—that's the possibility. But it's not going to crash and burn because I cheated."

Kujo patted my shoulder then turned to point a mug at me. "Coffee?"

"No, thanks. I want something a little—"

"Hex found something." Hermes called from the door. "You two having another hard conversation?"

Kujo shook his head. "Nah. We good."

"You sure?" Hermes asked. "Because I have a strong feeling I'm gonna have to have a talk with you and the rest of the guys."

"We're sure." I assured Hermes. "Kujo and I are good. Besides, what you said is true. I'm in this with you. Even though the others might object, you know what you want and I'm getting there."

Hermes stepped in and kissed my head and the three of us left the room to talk with Hex.

Soon, Hermes and I were speeding through the street in a black truck. Though we didn't speak, when I reached over and laced my finger with his free hand, Hermes didn't pull away. I exhaled and settled into the drive, until he pulled the truck into a parking spot at the side of the road.

After he fed the meter, he took my hand again and led me along the store-lined street. A red and white streetcar made its way in the opposite direction followed by cars and a lone motorcycle. He stopped suddenly and peered down an alley. The walls of the alley were covered in beautiful graffiti almost as if someone had taken the time to make sure they were perfect. We passed a few people taking photos, stopping briefly for them to get the shot they wanted before we hurried by.

We stopped at the end of the alley that split off into three directions. He glanced up which made me do the same. All I saw was blue sky, the CN Tower, and the smallest tip of an apartment building.

"This way." We went left and soon we arrived at a small, out of the way diner.

Hermes caught me around the hips pulled me into his chest and kissed me. I wanted to complain, that this wasn't the time or place to get freaky. Footsteps moving toward us caught my attention and me something was wrong.

He spun us around so that my back was to the

wall, and kissed me deeply, pressing his body intimately to mine.

For a moment, I'd forgotten we were on a mission.

In that space and time, I was Hermes' girl, and we were doing something very naughty.

But the footsteps didn't last forever. Too soon, they died in the distance and Hermes pulled away.

"Hold that thought." His voice cracked as he looked over his shoulder.

"That was Solva." He told me.

"We should go after him!" I took his hand and tugged.

Hermes didn't move. "Following him downtown Toronto isn't safe and too complicated with traffic. We know where he'll be. We either have to smoke him out when we're ready or go in and get him."

I exhaled. "Time for the calvary?"

Hermes smiled and kissed me again until my knees wobbled beneath me. I clutched his hips.

"For sure." He replied when he finally lifted his head. "Let's order food for the others. We can't take down Troy on an empty stomach."

"Um—didn't they use a giant horse for that?"

"Amateurs." Hermes teased.

I laughed.

Hermes lifted his cell to his ear. While he waited, I stuck my head out into the path and looked both ways. People were still taking pictures.

"Hex." Hermes' voice pulled my gaze to his handsome face. "We found it…yeah. We're heading back."

Since the next time we would be back in the alley, it would be for a whole entirely different reason, I had Hermes take some pictures of me there. We also did a few selfies, and I couldn't remember ever feeling that sexy before.

In the pictures, he held my hips, kissed my neck, carried me on his back—I didn't wan this to end.

TIANNA SHARP

WHILE WE WAITED for the Titan brothers and Echo to arrive, Kujo went for a run. Hermes and sequestered ourselves in his office. He gave me use of his computer and I began by checking my emails.

I shouldn't have.

Since I'd left home, I hadn't bothered checking. And since my phone could be used to track me, it had been on airplane mode and off the entire time. Usually, I lived on the thing. But the risk was far to great to disobey. Turning it on could cost me Hermes and I wasn't about to take that chance.

While he read from a book on the leather sofa, I tried focusing on work. I began by setting an out of office message. Then, I started going down the list of over two hundred emails. Most of them, so far, were pricing questions, a few of them seemed sketchy but I flagged them and carried on.

From time to time, I glanced up at Hermes. There was something sexy about a man who read Tolstoy.

"War and Peace?"

"Mmhmm."

"Do you like it?" I asked.

"So far."

"Would you think of me differently if I told you I was supposed to read it in college and couldn't get through it?"

Hermes looked up and smiled at me. "No. This kind of work isn't for everyone." He went back to his book.

Sighing, I tried focusing again on my emails. Though it was a struggle, I waded through quite a few before I gave in.

Sending one final email, I logged out of everything and made my way over. I climbed into his lap and cuddled into his chest.

Most men would have complained. They would have told me how busy they were and how distracting I was being. But Hermes was different. He paused to shift me comfortably against him, kissed me between the eyes then went back to his book.

I sighed and closed my eyes. Being like this with him was strangely invigorating. His arms were the like the perfect safety blanket—warm and perfect.

After a while, I fell asleep.

When I opened my eyes, outside the window as dark. Hermes was lying behind me with me cuddled into his body and a blanket over us. I didn't want to move but something had caused me to open my eyes.

Blinking, I remained still, waiting for a reminder.

"Hermes?" Kujo's voice was close to the door now.

When he stepped into the room, I groaned and tried sitting up. Hermes tightened his arms around me.

"Five more minutes." He moaned.

"I'd love to, but Kujo is here." I told him.

"I know Kujo is here." Hermes told me. "Go back to sleep."

Smiling, I kissed Hermes' nose. "No, I mean, he's in the office with us."

Hermes shifted but didn't open his eyes. "Are they here?" He asked.

"Yeah," Kujo said.

I shoved my feet off the sofa and tucked the blanket behind me. Kujo must have guessed my struggle for he extended a hand to me to help me onto my feet. Smiling, I thanked him then turned to poke Hermes who bit toward me.

"You're grumpy after you wake up." I accused.

He merely winked at me and pushed from the sofa.

When I finally entered the room with the others after using the bathroom, the room was full. I recognized Echo and Knight, but the other man, I assumed was Knight's brother who they called Thunder. He was a photocopy of Knight, dark skin, shaved head, full lips, flat nose—sexy.

"You must be Tianna." Thunder extended a hand. "Roan Titan—they call me Thunder."

I shook his hand. "It's a pleasure. Though I wish it was under better circumstances."

He smiled at me and I fell into the seat beside Hermes.

"Echo, if you're here, who's running Crosshairs?" I asked her.

"My sister." Echo grinned. "I owe her big. She had to cancel a date to do that and apparently the guy didn't take it very well. Tinder dates are so shallow."

"Oh—maybe I could help?" I told her. "You know? Help you make it up to her? Then again, from the way the guy reacted to her cancelling, we may be doing her a favor."

"She loves your clothes…" Echo pointed out.

"Say no more." I giggled. "When this is over, she is welcome to fly in and raid my storeroom."

"Don't say that unless you mean it." Echo arched a brow.

"My showroom has two floors." I pointed out. "I have clothes in there no one in the world has seen before. Trust me, I will pay for her flight and everything. Don't even worry about it."

Echo flailed.

The others laughed.

We began planning the end of Solva's world.

They kept the plan simple—which was good for me. Echo and Knight would go into the club and root Solva out. We were pretty sure he'd try going out the second exit that led up into the diner. I wanted him alive and I told them so, and as we sped through the night, I wondered why.

We arrived at a parking spit and I decided I just wanted him out of my life. I didn't care how. He'd taken my brother over a chip that didn't belong to him. Someone had betrayed Montana and his guys for money and all that caused me to pull Hermes and his friends away from their lives.

On second thought, I want to punch Solva in the dick—

—hard.

While the others set up and got into position, Kujo sat with us, watching while Hermes showed me again how to use the handgun. Though it weighed like the galaxy now sitting in the holster Hermes had strapped to my hips, I didn't have a choice. I had to protect myself and Hermes probably wouldn't worry if he knew I had a weapon. I nodded and as I reached in for a kiss, Kujo climbed out the back of the truck.

Hermes was next to climb out and I turned to watch him stick money into the meter. He was dressed in all black and when he walked back toward me, I couldn't help thinking he moved like a demon.

I licked my lips and scrambled from the vehicle,

pulled my light jacket around me to hide the weapon and reached for his hand.

"How are you guys doing?" Hex asked in our earpieces.

Everyone chimed in.

"We're in." Thunder's voice was strong. "How about you guys?"

"Almost." Hermes replied. "We're entering now."

Kujo backed off.

Hermes and I entered alone.

Silence—as we stepped through the small purple door and into what looked like a regular diner. I wish we could just ask where the secret entry was, but I supposed we'd find out soon enough.

The woman at the counter flipping through a magazine told us to sit anywhere without looking up. We were the only ones there—which wasn't weird. I was curious how they made their money if no one knew the diner was there. Then again, enough tourist coming down the alley to take pictures of the graffiti may have been the place's saving grace.

We sat at a table where Hemes could see every part of the place without turning. I sat beside him and scooted into his side. It would look less suspicious if they thought were dating.

Kujo didn't enter and I figured he was the backup.

The rude waitress arrived, popping her gun while dropping menus in front of us. I looked down on them wondering if they'd fall apart if I touched them.

She remained there, loudly chomping on the gum and popping bubbles large enough to block her face. Usually, I'd call her on her shit, but maybe another time. I ordered soda to drink, then settled for the Reuben sandwich with French fries on the side. I wasn't really hungry—it was the only thing that didn't seem like an outright waste of food when we left.

After Hermes' order, she walked away, and I rolled my eyes and settled heavily against him. He kissed my head, but I knew his mind was on the fight we would have ahead.

I snuggled close to him and kissed his neck until he moaned.

"Woman." He growled, gripping my arm. "I'll punish you later."

I giggled. "You promise?"

He smirked and kissed my nose as the waitress returned with our drinks, said nothing and went off again.

"What's chomping at her ass?" I grunted.

"Not today, Anna."

"I know."

"He's here now." Echo's voice came through the earpiece.

I'd almost forgotten they were there. Sighing softly, I looked down at my glass, needing the cold, carbonated taste of soda to lift my mood a little. But the glass didn't look clean and I just couldn't get myself to drink from it.

"Asshole." I muttered.

Nothing seemed to be going my way. Something as simple as a damn glass of soda was a problem. I used a fingernail to ease the glass away from me.

"Any idea where the stairs may be?" I pretended to be nipping at Hermes' ear.

"I don't think its in the kitchen." Hermes bowed his head to kiss my lips. "I'm thinking in the basement—in downtown places like this, the bathrooms are usually down there. That way it wouldn't look suspicious if he's coming up the stairs."

"Guys, get ready." Knight warned.

"Kujo?" Hermes called.

"I'm here." Kujo replied.

"Did you get that?" Thunder wanted to know.

"Loud and clear." Kujo told us.

It wasn't long afterward that the world erupted into bangs and booms. Hermes and I shot from the seating but didn't move toward where the gunshots were coming from. Instead, he shifted backward as a group of men bolted from up a set of stairs at the far end of the place and headed for the door.

I recognized Solva—tall, a side of his face scarred.

The men around him seemed to be shielding him as he took off out the door. Hermes and I followed. Footsteps behind me caught my attention and I swung around to find Knight, Echo and Thunder chasing after us.

Outside, we found Kujo standing with his gun to Solva's head.

"Well, well," Kujo said. "You look pretty good for a dead man."

"And you've gotten old." Solva spat. "Kill him!"

"You might want to look behind you." Kujo told him. "For shits and giggles—take a look. Go on."

Solva shifted on his feet to face us. The moment he realized what had happened, I could see the rage in his eyes.

I stepped to Hermes' side.

"Your brother couldn't leave well enough alone." Solva spat. "I wish I could kill him more than once."

Angry, I aimed my gun at him.

Solva laughed. "What're you going to do with that? Little girl, please." He turned to face Kujo again.

"I'm going to need you to look at me." I swallowed the lump in my throat.

"Don't you see the men are talking!" Solva snapped.

"I need you to look at me." I jabbed him in the back with the end of the gun. "When I shoot you in the head, I want you to see it coming. Turn —around!"

Solva had an almost bored look on his face.

My anger flared higher.

"Tell me who sold you information on the Protectors." I told him.

Joseph was dead and I knew why he died and who killed him. Solva didn't have anymore answers for me. But I would make sure I protected Montana and his guys with the new power I found myself with.

"Fuck you." He replied.

"No, thank you." I spat, jamming him in the chest with the gun. "I'm good. Who gave you the information on the Protectors?"

"Like I said, fuck you."

"So, *fuck you* is your final answer then?" I asked.

When he said nothing, I lowered the gun and shot him in the knee. The gunshot echoed throughout the alley as he hit the ground. One of his goons stepped toward me and Echo caught him by the back of the neck and brought her gun down over head.

The man slumped to the ground, unconscious.

The others seemed to have learned their lesson—especially as Kujo jammed his gun to one of their chests.

"Who's next?" Echo asked.

"You shot me!" Solva screeched. "You fucking shot me!"

"Let me explain something to you." I aimed toward his other knee. "Those men mean the world to me. And you and your asshole friends went for them. Not only that, you killed my brother. So, technically, I have nothing else to lose. I'm only going to ask one more time—" I changed my aim to his crotch.

"Guys, whatever you're doing," Hex said. "Do it fast. It's getting kinda hard fielding all the 9-1-1 calls about your shenanigans."

"Anna?" Hermes' called my name, but I didn't look away.

"Stop her!" Solva called.

"Solva, we don't live in the middle ages anymore." Kujo teased. "Women are allowed to vote now—make up their own minds."

"You brought this on yourself." Knight pipped up. "You know what happens when someone comes for our brothers and sisters. We react—most often than not, adversely."

"You killed my brother." I reminded him. "He may have been a piece of shit, but he was *my* piece of shit. He was the only family I had left. And thanks to you, he's gone. I'd like to pay you back for all the trouble you've caused me. A bullet to the dick seems like an appropriate way of repaying your kindness. What do you think, Solva?"

"I think she's serious." Thunder muttered.

Solva covered his dick with his hand as if he thought that would stop a bullet. "It's Ozzy!" He shouted. "Oh, God, please! It was Ozzy, okay?"

"Name sounds familiar, Kujo?" I asked.

"Oh yeah." Kujo replied.

"What're we doing with him?" Thunder wanted to know.

"We take him with us." Kujo told us. "I need to take him back across the border.

"He's going into the trunk." Hermes told us. "He's not going into my car bleeding like that."

"And them?" I asked.

The others worked to disarm the men and sent them on their way. Hermes was pretty sure they wouldn't talk to anyone. Bottom feeders were loyal, or they wouldn't get picked up by the next wealthy asshole.

Knight took off for one of the vehicles and when he returned, we loaded Solva in it and slammed the trunk.

Hermes took the weapon from my hand and put it away. He then sat in the back seat while Thunder drove us back to the home we'd been staying at. With Solva restrained, Kujo and I cleaned his wound, ensuring he wouldn't bleed to death while we waited for the doctor Knight had connections with.

The man arrived to look at the wound, ensured it was cleaned properly and tried giving Solva pain medication.

"He gets nothing." I told the doctor. "Let him suffer."

"Getting shot is painful." The doctor pleaded.

"I'm sure." I folded my arms. "Let him hurt. Maybe

then he'll know how I felt when I found out my brother was dead."

The doctor turned to look at Solva, then over at Kujo. Eventually, he gathered his things and pushed to his full height. He handed me a bottle. "He may get a fever when the body begins fighting to keep his wound from getting infected. If that happens, give him one tablet every four hours until the fever dies."

I wrapped my fingers around the bottle and storm by Kujo.

That fool killed my brother. I wanted him to die, not be his nurse.

I sighed.

MAKSIM DEMIDOV

FOR THE NIGHT, Tianna had curled up into my arms. She didn't sleep a wink. I wasn't sure what to say to her to make it all better. Instead, I remained awake with her. A few times I tried crawling out of bed to check on Solva, but she wouldn't let go. I simply kissed her head and remained by her side.

When sunlight began streaming through the window, she climbed out of bed and closed herself off in the bathroom.

I hurried down the hall to use one of the other bathrooms. Finally dressed, I checked on Solva to see he was still cuffed to the bed. I felt his forehead, but he wasn't having a fever.

Leaving him, I found Kujo in the living room on the phone to his lady.

I waved at him then entered the kitchen to pour

myself some coffee and grabbed an apple from the pile on the counter. I sipped on the coffee and waited for Kujo to finish his call.

"I fed him." Kujo said. "There's breakfast in the oven."

"Thanks, but I'm not hungry." I settled in the sofa and placed the apple on the center table. "I'll give you the jet to take him back. You can't exactly walk into Pearson and catch a flight."

Kujo smiled. "I told Montana about Ozzy."

"Who's this Ozzy?" I asked.

"A new hire." Kujo replied. "When we brought him in, Reaper was not impressed. He didn't like him from the moment their eyes met."

"Did he give a reason?"

"Said Ozzy gave him a bad feeling." Kujo chuckled. "And Reaper didn't like his face."

"Seems I need to meet this cat." I joked.

Kujo sighed and took my coffee away to sip from the mug. "Ugh! How do you drink this?"

I laughed.

"I think you should check your nipples for hair or something."

"Don't be dramatic." I laughed harder. "You can add milk or cream or whatever to yours."

"Dramatic?" Kujo asked. "Brother, I feel like I need to shave my tongue." Kujo stuck his tongue out while raking his teeth over it. "What brand of coffee is that?"

"It's called Jardin."

"Christ on a cracker that's strong." He tapped his lips as though he thought that would take the taste out of his mouth then exhaled loudly. "How's Tianna holding up?"

"She's angry." I replied. "Other than that, I think she'll be okay. She wanted to kill him."

"No offence, but we all want that toad dead."

"It's more than that." I set my mug down and flopped back in my seat. "This man has taken from her—sure, Joseph was an ass, but he was her brother. I don't think she was prepared for the pain having Solva at her mercy like that would have caused."

"I have a weird question." I leaned back and rubbed my eyes for a moment. "And I'd like to think I've never been a vain man. But…"

"And you were never the man to beat around the bush either." Kujo pointed out.

I chuckled. "Do you think Tianna is still in love with Montana?"

"The honest answer is, I don't know." Kujo replied. "If I was being completely straight with you, I don't think she ever really loved him. You can't cheat on someone you love and besides, like I said before, they were too young to be that serious. We all get into those relationships we think is going to last forever. Most often than not, we go in for all the wrong reasons."

"Like?"

"I don't know." Kujo shrugged. "We see something shinny and think it's gold. Then the rain comes, and we realize—fool's gold."

"Kujo…"

"You do understand what I mean, right?"

I nodded. "It wasn't real to begin with."

"That's right."

His words echoed through my head and played back to him repeatedly. What if what I was feeling for her was fool's gold? There were no guarantees when it came to love and the by products of love.

"And." Kujo's voice cut through my thoughts and I looked over at him. "Even if she is, nothing will come of it. Listen, she's here with you, isn't she?"

"But is that because she had to?"

"I'm sure it started out that way."

I nodded in agreement and understanding.

"But the two of you have been spending a lot of time together. She's seen the way you react to things, has had a chance to look at you—truly look at you." Kujo cleared his throat. "That's when the realness of whatever you're both feeling begins to set in. The real, true feelings come from moments together— times when you're both unguarded."

"You sound like a romance novel."

Kujo smiled. "I got the girl, didn't I?"

"You got the girl." I chuckled.

"Listen to me, brother." Kujo met my gaze. "As men, we sit around, and we talk shit. We say things like, *I just don't understand women.* And, *women are so complicated.* They're not really. See, all women want is for us not be complete dicks. They want us to love them, take out the garbage once in a while and put down the toilet seat. See? Not complicated at all."

I laughed softly. "When you put it like that."

"What I'm trying to say is this." Kujo leaned back. "Don't overthink this. If you and Tianna are going to work, you can't bring Montana into the mix. He's moved on, the world went back to spinning right. Let Tianna find that peace. If you can't get over the fact that she was with Montana first, then you need to walk away."

"I can't walk away." I admitted. "But thinking she might still have something for Montana—it drives me crazy."

"Look, here are my two cents." Kujo leaned in. "There is a risk in every relationship. After all, sometimes they don't work out and it sucks. But that's life. What the two of you need to do, is lay your cards on the table—all of them. Figure out what you are to each other and what you want from each other, then go from there. If it works, I'll dance at your wedding. If not, you lick your wounds and try again."

Before I could speak again, Tianna joined us and after she was caffeinated, we set to work plotting how to get Solva out of the country and back in US hands. After Hex booked the flight with my private jet, I gave Tianna her phone back. She turned it on, and all the messages began coming through.

She moaned and turned it off again.

"I'm going to shower," Kujo told us.

He winked at me and left the room.

"Um—can you take a walk with me?" I asked her.

Tianna stared at me, suspicion filling her gaze. Still, she rose and nodded.

We exited the home and headed along Kingston Road toward the lake. For a while, we said nothing. The warm breeze swirling silently around us and the trees. Cars zoomed back and forth to our left, and the sound of a dog barking in the distance reminded me I wasn't in the confines of the house anymore.

"What now?" I asked as we crossed the street to head down Brimley.

"I don't know." She replied. "It's not like I have to learn how to live without my brother. I lost him years ago when he decided to pick himself up and move to Canada."

"I was actually being selfish." I admitted. "I was asking what about us. I guess what I'm asking first of all is, is there an us?"

"There's an us."

"You should take your time answering that question."

"Why?" Tianna glanced up at me then turned her attention ahead again. "Men always say women don't know what they want. You don't have that problem,

Hermes. You have a woman right here, who knows precisely what she wants."

"And what's that?"

"You."

My feet stopped moving even though my brain wanted them to keep going. I stared after her, the proud way her steps carried her away from me. I loved the way her back arched then sloped down into her ass. And the way her ass moved beneath the fabric of her—

"You coming?" Tianna called.

I jogged to catch up with her. When I fell into step beside her, my brain was still stuck on that one word.

You.

"I want to stay." Tianna stopped to face me. "When I was a little girl, my mother told me one of the reasons she knew my father was the one, was that when he was with her, she felt invincible. No matter the danger or the worry—she knew he would never leave her."

"I don't know if—"

"When she was telling me all that, I thought for sure she was lying." Tianna scoffed. "No man could ever make a woman feel that safe. But then I came here and my safest moments were the times I curled myself into your arms. Does that make me weak? I've tried being a strong, independent woman but Hermes…"

"Wanting my arms doesn't take away your independence or your strength." I encouraged her. "Wanting a man—*your* man to take care of you won't either. I want to be that for you."

"And my work?" She asked. "I know most rich men don't want their women doing anything."

He scoffed. "I get the feeling trying to stop you from working would be like trying to stop the world from turning. I'm not interested in taking anything away from your life, Anna. I want to add to it. And I just thought you could do with a very sexy arm candy on your arm."

She laughed out loud and smacked my shoulder. "Stop that."

"Seriously, though—I love that you *need* nothing from me. But I want you to want me."

"But I do want something from you." Tianna winked at me.

Every part of me wanted her and I didn't want to fight it anymore.

"You're quiet." She whispered.

"You're beautiful."

Tianna gasped softly and turned her face away. "Maksim."

"Wait—has no one ever told you you're beautiful before?"

"No. I've never been the kind of woman who needs to hear that."

"It's not that you need to hear it." I told her. "No

one *needs* to hear it. It's a matter of your man appreciating you, I—Tianna, you are so beautiful."

I framed her face.

Tianna sighed and kissed my neck.

"You said you wanted something from me—what's that?"

She giggled, kissed my neck then grabbed my dick.

"Tianna Sharp! You bad girl." I growled at her.

"Is that a yes?"

"Anytime you want it." I replied, my body already throbbing for more of her. But I had to wait.

"I'll have to fly back to Montana to get a few things straight." She released me but didn't step away. "Want to come and be my cowboy for a bit?"

I laughed. "Cowboy?"

"Before you agree." She took my hand and we continued toward the water's edge. "You'll have to wear the hat and the assless chaps."

"Easy access? Ms. Sharp, what kind of man do you think I am?"

She giggled. "Seriously though, I'll need a workspace, maybe a showroom…"

"Have you ever thought of opening your own store?"

"My own store…"

"Yeah. I mean, you can still do your regular stuff." I told her. "But your brand could be out there, people walking into your own spot, picking up your designs."

"I have thought about it." She sighed. "But it would be hard. I mean, coming here took me out of the game. I have a lot to face once I focus on work again."

"But it's not impossible."

"It's not." She seemed thoughtful until she smiled. "But you know something – we don't have to make that decision today."

Tianna stopped again.

This time she pulled her body against mine and I tangled my arms around her. After a deep kiss that made me hard and wanting to push her against a nearby tree and tear her clothes off, she looked up into my eyes and smiled.

"Once Kujo is in the air with his cargo, you and I will go on a date—a real one."

"Does that mean we hold hands then you see how far I'll let you go?" Tianna playfully walked two fingers up my arm.

I wiggled my brows at her and she giggled again.

Just as we were walking through the door again, my phone rang. Tianna left me with a kiss and disappeared into the kitchen. When I checked and saw it was Montana, my heart did a strange, painful flip.

I answered it.

"Can we talk?" Montana asked.

I wasn't stupid enough to not know this was

coming. It was as clear as the nose on my face it would—I thought I had more time.

I exhaled heavily. "Of course."

Instead of following Tianna, I entered my office and closed the door. When I was in my chair, I cleared my throat. "I supposed you want to talk about Tianna."

"Yes."

"You two aren't together anymore." I spoke. "You haven't been together in a very long time."

"Hermes, I only want to make sure you're going into this with open eyes."

"My eyes are open, trust me." I assured him. "I feel things for her and from her that tell me this is good—this feels right."

"All right. Kujo tells me he's bringing back a gift."

"Yeah. Tianna wanted to kill him." I told Montana. "The strange thing is, I think she was angry about her brother but the fact this guy wanted to come after you..."

"She's always been like that." Montana replied. "That's why her cheating had stunned me so much. I really hope she's different, Hermes. I want to believe we didn't work because we were so young and we weren't meant to. I mean, if things had gone the way I wanted them, I wouldn't have met Sadie."

"And she wouldn't have been here with me." I nodded.

We chatted for a while longer until he asked to

have a talk with Kujo. After I handed off the phone, I joined Tianna in her bedroom, pulling her into my side on the bed. Silently, we remained with each other, my heart beating faster and faster.

Being with a woman had never scared me before. But with Tianna, my whole world felt as if it had been upended, rattled and set right again. I was leaning in for a kiss when Kujo knocked and poked his head into the room to return my phone.

"Call Echo back," he said and left us alone again.

Curious, I called Echo. She didn't really want to speak to me. Her sister didn't believe Echo knew Tianna and wanted proof.

"We'll swing by Crosshairs tomorrow," Tianna said. "I can meet her then."

"Sure, what time?" Echo wanted to know.

"Lunch?" Tianna looked up at me.

I nodded. "We'll swing by at lunch."

Echo cheered and when she was finally gone, I placed the phone on the bedside table.

"Hermes?"

"Hmmm?"

"I need a favor." Tianna sat up to look down at me.

"Sure…"

"Actually, I need two favors." She smirked.

I grunted.

"One, shopping. I need more than the clothes I

have right now. You just have to sit back and tell me what you think looks cute on me."

"Um…" I glanced down at the front of my pants. "Someone likes that idea."

She laughed and smacked my shoulder. "Behave."

"And the second favor…"

"That one is a little more immediate." Tianna toyed with one of my nipples through my shirt. "Do you get it?"

"Say it out loud." I teased. "Call its name."

She bit into her bottom lip and climbed over me. I watched as she lifted her shirt over her head. The lace of her bra rested on beautiful flesh—flesh I knew to be soft and fragrant.

Unable to stop myself, I dragged my palms up her sides, along her curves until I could finally cup her breasts in my palms.

Tianna moaned and tossed her head back. She rolled her hips against me, crushing my confined arousal under her. I Wanted to devour her, consumed her, claim her. All of her should belong to me and I felt no shame or guilt about it.

"Tianna." I sighed.

She leaned forward and kissed me, one that curled my toes and aroused every part of me.

Rolling over, I pressed her into the bed while restraining her wrists above her head with one of my palms. I rooted around in the drawer of the bedside table until I found a pair of scissors then proceeded to cut the soft lace of her bra from her body.

My name tumbled from her lips like water, but I was too far gone to really hear much else. Her nipple tightened against my tongue.

This feels right.

She's mine—and I'm not letting go.

THE ROUGHNESS of his facial hair on my nipples made my thighs shake. I was powerless when he took my body like this, his strength pressing me into whatever surface he had me on. My body sank backward into the bed as he drove into me. Hermes grabbed me in the way I craved—my thighs, my ass, my shoulders— he handled me like a man should.

I gasped, arched my body and looked up into his eyes. There was something about the way Hermes looked at me that had me feeling sexier than any woman had a right to feel. I melted for him, moaned for him and came roughly because of him.

Shaking, I slumped backward, deeper into the bed as I caught the cross of his pendant between my teeth. Hermes growled for me and every part of me responded to the primal sound.

"Please…" I sighed.

Hermes pulled away from me and turned me face down. Immediately I stuck my ass up to accept him from behind. He nibbled at my shoulder, my ear, the back of my neck as he surged inside me again. This time, I shoved my face into the pillows and cried out to him.

Good.

So good.

His breathing was rough—carnal, hot. I mewled each time he exhaled on my skin and rode backward to accept him.

Maksim Demidov was mine.

He was the man I wanted to be with, to have love me every night as I climbed into his bed. I needed his strength, his rawness, his kind eyes.

With that thought, I gave myself completely over to everything he offered.

I opened myself up for him to take what he needed from me and I felt no guilt or shame about it. This was a new kind of love I'd never felt before. It flooded my veins like fire, and I didn't think I'd be able to go on without it.

"Mine…" I whispered just before another orgasm surged through me.

"What is?" Hermes asked.

"You."

He came then, roughly, slamming into me until his entire body stiffened on top of me.

"You are mine." I repeated it a little clearer.

Hermes moaned and fell heavily against my back. His breathing loud and hot. I turned my face to get it across my cheek and nose. He kissed my cheek then my ear.

"I think my body likes the sound of that." He panted. "I like the sound of that."

We made love again then settled in each other's arms. As the daylight began slowly vanishing, I shifted against him. "I'm curious."

"Okay?" Hermes caressed my arm up and down again.

"How do you make your money?"

"The bulk of it came from my grandfather." He replied. "He moved here from Russia when he was twenty and worked as a janitor for twelve years. He was lucky enough to invest in a computer company. I mean, playing the market is always unpredictable and very few people make money from it. He was one of the lucky ones—withing a couple of years he owned his own tech firm. When he died, he left me the bulk of his estate."

"What about your father?"

"My father had his issues." He explained. "He was never any good with money. Grandfather left him some money but not as much as he thought he should have gotten. Though my grandfather was against it, I set up a trust-fund for my father. When I was twenty-seven, he allowed his new girlfriend to talk him into heading to the motherland."

"Okay?"

"Her and her family had him murdered to get his money."

"Oh, Maksim—I'm so sorry."

"It's okay. It's been a while." He replied.

"Did the cops catch them?" I wanted to know.

"No," he said. "I knew the law wouldn't do anything. So, I waited. It was only a matter of time until she realized my father had squandered his money and was living off money she wouldn't have access to. A month later one of her brothers took a shot at me."

"What?"

"I'm still standing." He brushed his lips against my forehead. "They aren't."

He didn't have to say much else. I knew what that meant. This woman and her brother or brothers were either dead or in a prison.

"The rest of my money comes from real estate investments and developments." He continued. "Tell me, you thought I was a part of the mafia, didn't you?"

"What?" I sat up to look at him. "No. Nothing like that—it's just, well, I was curious."

He smiled and caressed my bare back. "What about you?"

"I went off to design school after high school." She replied. "I guess they realized I had some talent because I began getting calls about designing for local celebrities. I made deals with Instagram models —they could wear one of my designs on red carpets or special things on their channel. Within a year, I was getting three to five orders per months. And this was before I even graduated."

"Wow."

"Yeah." She curled her legs under her. "I made my money the old fashion way, I'm afraid. Blood, sweat and tears—quite literally."

He shifted forward to kiss my knee then flopped back into the pillows. As I stared down at him, I couldn't help marvelling about how sexy he truly was. The soft hairs on his chest brought back memories of them sliding over my nipples, making me wet and craving all he had to give me.

Maksim Demidov

THE ONLY MOVEMENT we made for the rest of the evening and the night was to use the bathroom and grabbed food. Kujo had gone out with the Titan brothers and echo, leaving us to babysit Solva. At one point, I went in with Tianna.

I said nothing but I didn't leave the room.

Over my dead body was that fool going to be alone with my woman. Though he was restrained, I strapped a holster around my right thigh and shoved a loaded Glock into it.

Tianna walked in and pulled up a chair to the bed to look into Solva's face. For a while, she said nothing. Solva turned his head and when he saw her, I'd never seen that man afraid of anyone before.

"You're afraid," Tianna said finally. "Good."

"Fuck you."

"That seems to be the extent of your vocabulary." Tianna smiled. "How eloquent."

"What do you want?"

"Did you kill my brother yourself or did you send someone to do it?" Tianna asked.

Solva said nothing.

Tianna lifted her arm and brought it slamming down into Solva's wound.

I winced as he screamed in pain.

"You're fucking crazy!" Solva sobbed.

"Crazy?" Tianna asked. "You think this makes me crazy? I asked you a question and you *will* answer it truthfully or as God is my witness, I will make you hurt more than you are hurting right now!"

Solva lunged at her but before I could react, Tianna had karate chopped him in the throat. He hit the bed again like wet sack of dirt.

"Try that again." Tianna growled. "I dear you."

If looks could kill…

"Did you kill my brother yourself or did you send someone to do it?" She asked again.

Her voice was raw, without emotion and for a moment, I worried.

"He was a special case." Solva squeaked. "I did it myself. He stole from me! Nobody steals from me! I made him suffer and I enjoyed every second if it!"

Tianna looked back at me for a second, evil dancing in her eyes. When she trapped him with her gaze again, she stood and leaned over. She dragged her hand down his thigh to his wound again and dug her fingers into it.

I'd never heard a cry like that before. Solva was hurting bad but I felt no sympathy for him. He'd done worse to Tianna and she was merely returning the favor.

"I told you everything!" Solva cried. "What more do you want?"

"From you?" Tianna asked. "Nothing—not really. I just want you to look at my face and remember it. I want every time you think of stepping out of line again, you think of me. You think of me aiming a gun at your junk and pulling the trigger. I want you to pay for all the shit you've pulled while on government contracts and all the evil you've helped into these two countries. And if for some reason you don't go down for your crimes, remember one thing. I have the money to find you. And next time, I'll be pulling the trigger."

Solva said nothing.

"Speak!" She snapped.

"I get it!" Solva sobbed.

Tianna pulled her hand back and it was covered in blood that had seeped through the bandage. Solva panted and kind of melted backward into the bed. His eyes widened as he lifted his free hand to cover his cock.

The pride I felt for Tianna then pushed a smile to my lips.

"Are you going to let her talk to me like this?" Solva called to me. "Let her do this to me? You were military, weren't you?"

"Let me?" Tianna asked. "You think the little lady needs her man's permission to kick your ass?"

"Now you've done it." I scoffed. "Listen, I'm just here to appease the alpha in me. I think we can both agree she doesn't need my permission for anything. But if you'd like, I can leave the room and let you two talk."

Solva swallowed and looked at Tianna who was stepping away from the bed. "I need something for the pain."

"You heard the lady." I told him. "You get nothing. The pain will do you good. Consider it a penance."

After we left the room, Tianna called the doctor to come back and take a look at Solva's leg. As angry as she'd been at him, I knew she didn't want him dying from an infection. She washed her hands and by the time she found me again, I was on a video call with Hex. She didn't seem to care and merely crawled into the sofa beside me and rested her head in my lap.

"Go." Hex told me. "She needs you."

I blew my friend a kiss and she was gone after a wink.

"Lover?" I called as I caressed her hair from her face. "Are you okay?"

"Not right now." She admitted.

"What can I do?"

"You're doing it." She leaned forward to kiss my stomach then settled back on my thigh. I caressed her cheeks, down her nose then dragged a thumb over her lips.

"I'm so proud of you."

"Proud that I'm splintering?" She asked.

"No." I dragged a palm down her shoulder and up again. "Proud that you stood up for your brother, stood up for yourself. Other women would have melted. They would have wavered when Solva called their bluff."

"But I wasn't strong, Hermes." She lifted brown eyes at me. "I was scared."

"Of course, you were scared. You're not a soldier. But you did what needed to be done for your brother. You stood toe to toe with a man like Solva and you put the fear of God in him. How can I not be proud?"

She sighed.

Though I took a few calls regarding the flight

back to Montana, I didn't move. Tianna used the bathroom and, in that time, I grabbed snacks from the kitchen. She returned and took up her position again, this time on her back for me to feed her cheese and grapes with my fingers.

Kujo found us like that a little later when he returned.

"Everything is set for the flight back to Montana." I told him. "Nine at night."

"I'll be ready."

Seconds ticked away into minutes which melted into hours until it was time for us to get Kujo to meet the private jet. Kujo flew out with Solva and when they landed at a private airstrip, Montana was there to greet them. Solva was handed over to the proper authorities to prepare him for his punishment and the world began ticking like it should again.

The hours ticked off into days and life was beginning to take on some sense of new normal.

After purchasing a new phone, Tianna dove into business to catch up on what she'd missed. Though she took on a few new projects, she seemed a bit shaky. I knew when she was thinking about her brother and Solva. In those moments, I wrapped my arms around her and took her away from work until she was breathing again.

"How she's doing?" Thunder asked while pouring me another drink.

I exhaled. "She's okay." I replied. "I think she's

afraid to set foot back in Montana right now. I'm not pushing."

"I thought you two were dating." Echo fell into the booth across from me.

"We are." I replied. "But she has a place and a business there. I don't want her giving up her life for mine. She wouldn't be happy with that."

"True, but if you guys get serious, that's a decision you both will have to make together." Knight added.

"We will. Right now, I want her to be steady before we tackle that." I sipped from my whiskey. "But we're planning on flying out in two weeks. Echo, will Tammy have time to go with us? Tianna wants to know if she'd like to come see the showroom."

"Listen, if Tammy has to sell her soul to the devil she will be on that plane." Echo laughed. "But let me go give her a call. Maybe she can swing by and make plans with Tianna when she comes for lunch?"

I nodded and Echo slipped out of the seat.

"Thanks for keeping our name out of the collar." Thunder spoke up.

"Of course." I told him. "You two were doing me a favour."

"Don't even. We were doing your lady a favor." Knight smirked. "We like her."

I tossed back my drink then chuckled. "Too bad she's taken."

"Better luck next time, I guess." Knight winked at me.

Echo returned with her arm looked with Tianna's. The two of them laughing and chatting about something. Tianna kissed me then slipped into the seat beside me.

"Let me tell the kitchen we're ready for lunch." Echo told us.

"We're not waiting for Tams?" Knight asked.

"She'll be here in ten minutes, she said when I spoke with her." Echo checked her watch. "I'll be back."

She'd closed down Crosshairs for the day so we could have time together. I didn't even realize the day our friendship became this close. The Titan brothers needed help, I had the means to and they came with Echo and Tammy. But I wouldn't change things for the world. They'd been there for me numerous times, though they had a reputation in the city of being the sort of men who could burn someone's entire world to the ground.

They were good men and Echo was an amazing friend.

Tammy announced her arrival by screaming Tianna's name from across the bar. Tianna looked at me and smiled. We hadn't gotten the chance to meet up because of Tammy's work. Though we'd planned on it, she picked up an extra shift at the hospital and jumped on it.

"I'm going to take it that's Echo's sister." Tianna stood to hug her.

"Yes," Tammy replied. "The cute one of the two. Oh my God, you're Tianna Sharp."

We all ate lunch together then Tianna took Tammy to another table to talk. I couldn't keep my eyes off her. I barely heard what they were saying at my table until Thunder poked me with the back of his dessert fork.

"She's coming back, brother." Thunder joked.

The others laughed out loud.

"I'm sorry." I managed.

"Don't be." Knight told me. "It looks good on you."

"It?" I asked.

"Love." Echo replied for him. "You're falling for her and I've never seen you like this."

"I've never felt like this." I admitted.

WE'D PLANNED on heading back to Montana before.

But Tammy wasn't able to get the time off. I was perfectly happy with that, as I didn't think I was ready to face the music.

After three months living with Hermes in Toronto, flying back into Montana felt strange. I'd hidden from the world in his arms. The past three months were filled with elegant parties, slow dancing to no music in his living room—sometimes after we'd made love on the floor.

Each night for the past three months, I ate dinner with him—when we didn't go out, we'd take turns cooking.

When I allowed myself to think about it—I was happy.

One morning I woke up to find Hermes gone and a newspaper sitting on the island. I poured myself some coffee and unfurled it. The front page was a picture of us, walking through Toronto's biggest malls, hand in hand with the headline, *Billionaire Maksim Demidov off market.*

I pressed my eyes closed for a moment, took a few sips from my coffee then refocused on the paper. The article speculated on how long we'd been dating. It spoke on how Hermes was close friends with the super wealthy Titan brothers who were suspected of being in some kind of Mafia.

I rolled my eyes and tossed the paper into the recycle bin, refilled my coffee and wandered through the house to my new office. It was a downstairs bedroom Hermes and Knight had worked into turning into my workspace.

After three weeks, Tammy had had enough of her not being able to take time off. Her anger stemmed from having worked almost eight months without approved time off. She'd wound up quitting.

Personally, I didn't think that was the best of ideas, but she promised me she'd just come back and get a new one.

Even as we descended the steps of the private jet in Montana, it didn't feel like home anymore. It was almost as if I was visiting for the first time and I couldn't understand it.

But Montana, Kujo and Six awaited us on the tarmac by a couple of SUVs. I glanced over at Hermes who took my hand as we walked toward the protectors. He seemed happy to be there, but my heart wouldn't stop pounding inside my ears, threatening to deafen me.

They greeted each other and I hunched down to scratch Six behind the ears. He seemed to have remembered me because he licked my chin and wagged his tail like crazy.

I giggled. "It's good to see you too, sir."

"He gets all the girls." Kujo teased.

"That's because he gorgeous. Right, boy? Right?" I stood and Kujo hugged me. "It's good to see you, Kujo."

Montana hugged me too, but it wasn't a long one. Without a word, he walked toward one of the SUVs and climbed in.

On the way back to my place, I had them stop so I could grab some groceries. While they waited in the car, Hermes leant me a hand. We didn't speak.

It was my fault.

I was so deep inside my own bullshit, I couldn't find the right words to give him. It was almost as if we were back at the beginning of our relationship and I hated myself for that.

I hated that my guilt of what happened between Montana and I was getting in the way.

I was letting it get in the way.

Back in the vehicles again, we continued on, the Crazy Mountains, rising in front of us like an immovable God, reminding me Montana was once a place I called home.

They parked in my driveway and we entered the house. While Hermes opened windows to get some air through the place, I carried Echo and Tammy up the stairs and showed them their rooms. Tammy's first action was to twirl dramatically and fall backward onto the bed.

I laughed softly.

"I'll make something for us to eat." I turned for the door.

Echo stopped me with a hand on my shoulder. "You okay?"

I nodded. "Fine. Why?

"This can't be easy for you."

"What can't be?"

"Being under the same roof with your past and your present." Echo led me from the room Tammy was in and to the room she'd be using. Once she closed the door, I sat on the edge of her bed. "Hermes has been silent, and I can feel you pulling into yourself."

"I don't mean to." Tears burned my yes.

"Then put on the brakes, lady." Echo told me. "Right now, you're in a house with your ex and the man who wants to love you. Right now, you're silent and he doesn't know what to say to you. He feels as if you're that way because you're still in love with Montana."

"He said that?"

"He doesn't have to say it." Echo sat beside me. "You just have to look in his eyes."

"Shit."

"Indeed."

I buried my face in my palms for a second, trying to temper the panic slowly ebbing to the surface. "I'm not in love with Montana."

"Say it again, Tianna. Maybe next time you'll believe it."

I frowned. "You know what—fuck you."

Surging from the bed, I headed for the door, but Echo caught my arm. "You're going to lose him."

"If he has a problem, he should talk to me instead of pouting in the corner like some little boy!"

"Seriously?" Echo asked. "And what exactly is he supposed to say? Huh? It's Montana or me—those are the words you wanna hear, right? Listen, this isn't a movie. This is the man who's falling for you hurting and you give zero fucks!"

"That's not fair!"

"You wanna talk fair?" Echo chuckled bitterly. "Let's talk fair. You've barely said two words to him since we got on the jet. I've been watching the both of you. He tried touching you and you flinched."

"I didn't flinch."

"Think whatever you want." Echo shook her head. "Do you want to fix this or are you going to keep disagreeing with everything I say?"

I huffed.

"You flinched." Echo repeated.

"Do you think he's having the talk with Montana?" I asked.

"Why?" Echo asked. "To settle your sense of being fought over by two men?"

"What?" I snapped.

"He won't have this talk with Montana." Echo was direct.

"Why not?"

"Montana didn't cheat." Echo japed me in the chest with a finger. "You did. Montana has moved on and Hermes know short of the end of the world, Montana is in love with his lady."

"If he can't trust me, this wont work." I told her.

"It's not about trust." Echo shrugged. "You've gone way beyond that. It's about your man feeling a little insecure right now and you're doing nothing to help. Sure, he's a man, and he's been groomed to not admit when he feels like the most important thing in his life is being ripped out from under him. But all you have to do is look at him."

"What am I supposed to do?"

"Talk to him."

"And say what?"

"If I have to tell you that, Tianna." Echo headed over to where she'd dropped her phone on the bed and picked it up. When she walked back toward me, she stopped. "You don't deserve him."

She left me alone then, trapped in my uselessness. Eventually, I charged through the house calling for Hermes. The others looked up at me, but Hermes wasn't with them.

"Where's Maksim?" I asked.

"Went for a walk with Six," Montana replied.

"You let him wander off by himself! He doesn't know the way."

"No," Kujo handed Montana a mug. "But Six does. What's your problem?"

"I'm fucking it up!" I admitted out loud. "Do you know which way he went?"

"East." Montana arched a brow.

I could tell he wanted to ask but I was out the door before he could. Finding Hermes was easy enough. He was playing with Six at a nearby park. Since there wasn't a dog park close, he was playing with Six in a secluded area, away from the three kids playing in the sand at the playground.

I watched as he tossed the ball and Six took off running for it.

"You're going to just stand there staring?" He asked.

Hermes hadn't turn around to see me. I supposed his time in the Canadian special forces gave him that need trick.

"Hermes," I said instead of answering. "I need to talk to you."

When he glanced back to me, the frustration was evident in his eyes. "What do you want?" He asked.

Six brought the ball back and dropped it at Hermes' feet, then stood there, tongue out, tail wagging. Hermes picked up the ball and threw it again.

"Do you really think I'm still in love with Montana?" I asked.

"What is this, huh?" He took his eyes off the military dog for a second—not nearly long enough for me to see what he was feeling.

"I'm not in love with Montana." I told him.

Six returned with the ball and Hermes threw it again.

"I'm sorry I made it seemed as if I didn't want you to touch me."

He waited until Six came back with the ball and this time, he held on to it. Hermes still didn't say anything to what I'd said.

"Maksim, please." I sighed. "I wasn't paying attention. I was inside my head. Coming back here has been hitting me a little differently, okay? You know I love your touch."

Six must have gotten frustrated so he jogged over to a tree, peed against the base of it then went sniffing around the bush line.

"The truth is, at first, yes, I thought we could maybe rekindle." I wrapped my arm around myself. "But finding out he's married to someone else, that nipped that in the bud for me. I wasn't in love with him—I just thought I should be because there was a past there."

"And with me?"

"With you it's different and it's new." I admitted. "But I'm going to need you to trust me. If you can't then we're not going to work."

"Trust…" Hermes tossed the ball.

Six took off after the bouncing orb.

Hermes walked in the direction the dog was and I followed. "You can't do that, can you?"

"I can trust you, Anna." He replied hunching down to scratch Six's head. "But I need you to tell me that I'm the only one. I know it may sound childish to you, but I don't share."

He stood again to face me.

Bravely, I stepped around him to brace my palms to his chest.

He stared down at my face, his heated breath bathing my skin as he read my eyes. "I spoke with Montana. He said that door—the door between you and him has been closed. You tell me the same thing and we can move on."

"It can't be that easy."

"Sure, it can." He attached Six's leash and stood again. "It can. Because you said I had to be able to trust you. So, tell me I'm the only one, that we're the only two people in this relationship."

"And your friends…"

"I gave them the same talk I'm giving you." His eyes were serious. "Two people in this relationship."

"Then—yes." I replied. "The door is closed. If I had been honest with myself, I would have accepted it had been closed even before that whole incident. I just—we're being completely honest here, right?"

He nodded but glanced down to Six then back at me.

"I want you." I placed myself in the open as we began walking away from the park. "Only you. You're my second chance, Hermes and I'm not stupid enough to just let you walk away. When you suggested I opened my own store, no one else even thought to mention that to me. It's like you believed I can do it even though I don't believe in myself. For years, fear has stopped me from growing. And one word from you and I find myself thinking of the possibilities."

"It's not that big of a deal. I think you can do great things. That's normal, right?"

I smiled. "Not as normal as you'd think. Some men break their women down when they think she can accomplish more than they ever will."

'Some men are stupid."

"All I'm saying." I chuckled. "Is that I know by looking in your eyes that I could leave you here and go searching a million miles away and still not find a man who looks at me like you do. I wouldn't find another man who believes in me like you—who touches me like you do. And I definitely wouldn't find a man who loves me like you do."

"Love?"

"Yes, Hermes. You love me." My heart soared. "You don't have to admit it now. I'll wait."

He licked his lips. "What about you?"

"I'm not afraid to tell you I've fallen for you." I winked at him over my shoulder as I hunched down to caress the top of Six's head then kissed him between the eyes. "You just have to be open to receiving it."

I walked off ahead of him, swaying my hips a little more than I normally would. When I glanced back, he hadn't moved.

His eyes were glued to my ass.

I giggled.

Yes, Maksim "Hermes" Demidov, you are mine and when we get a chance alone, I'll show you what's yours.

EPILOGUE

Maksim Demidov

THE SOFT SCRATCHES of pencil over paper caught my attention. It was familiar sound to wake up to. Over the past few weeks, Tianna had gone back to work. She'd put on one major show so far in Toronto where Tammy was her lead model.

So much for Tammy going back to nursing.

With that show, Tianna had spent a lot of time early in the mornings before I woke, sketching.

Though I knew she was probably in her usual spot, I moaned and reached across the bed. My hand hit empty bed and I opened one eye. When I pushed to sit up, Tianna was sitting at the edge of the bed, with her new sketchpad open while she mercilessly wielded a pencil.

"You had a long night." My voice cracked. "Why are you not in bed?"

"You looked so good sleeping." Tianna didn't even look up. "I wanted to do this before you woke up."

I pushed upward, using one hand to drag two of the pillows up to rest behind my back. When I said nothing, she looked up then turned the sketchpad to show me what she'd been working on. It was a picture of me.

"Uh…"

"Why do you look so shocked?" She asked. "I told you I found you sexy."

"Is that how you see me?" I asked.

Tianna turned the picture back to look down at it. It seemed like an eternity passed before she moved or breathed. I allowed her the silence—sometimes a person needed quiet to dig through the riddles in their heads.

When her shoulders fell, I extended a hand to her. "Put the sketchpad down, Anna. Come back to bed."

For a moment I thought she would decline. Then I smiled at her and as she melted for me, Tianna closed the book and set it along with her pencil on the floor. She uncurled herself to place the sketchpad on the chair by the window then walked across the room toward me.

She looked so damned good in red.

I exhaled, licked my lips and kept my eyes on the way the soft material flowed over her body as she crawled into bed with me. She cuddled against me, one leg tossed over my thigh as she rested her ear over my heart.

"Sometimes I wake up, scared you're a dream." She shifted loser and I kissed her head. "I'll rest my head over your heart and listen to the beats, counting them, letting them put me back to sleep."

"It's been almost year, Anna." I whispered. "I promised you I was in that day we walked Six."

"I know. But a part of me still feels like I don't deserve you."

"What brought this on?"

Tianna cleared her throat and sat up. The satin nightgown she wore rose up her thighs and one of the straps fell down her shoulder. Unable to help myself, I dragged a palm from her shoulder, down her arm then skimmed a nail against her thigh.

Her flesh soft.

"All this time with me—have you been happy?" She asked me instead of answering.

"Yes."

"Are you sure?" She asked.

"Tianna, what's going on?"

The look in her eyes worried me. And when she said nothing, I sat up again to reach for her. Instead, she hopped from the bed.

"Stay right here." She said, her voice shaking.

"But—"

She was out the door before I could say anything. It's been a while now since she moved to live with me. The legalities took some time, but we weren't worried about it. Maybe she was having second thoughts.

I sighed and picked up my phone to check the messages. I was on my fourth text when she entered again, her hands behind her back. To give her my undivided attention, I set the cell down again and turned to hang my legs over the side of the bed to face her. She walked between my thighs and kissed me gently.

"So—since you've been happy, and I've been happy…" She set a velvet box on my thigh.

"Tianna…"

"Open it."

I lifted the lid and inside was a silver wring. I smiled before meeting her worried gaze. "Tianna?"

"Hmm?"

"Is this an engagement ring?" I asked. "Are you asking me to be your very own Trickster?"

"Yes." She replied. "I know this isn't done—"

"Forget what's done." I told her. Gently, I hooked my right index finger beneath his chin and tipped her head up. "Ask."

Tianna swallowed. "Will you marry me?"

I set the ring box on the bed and framed her neck with my palms. Her eyes filled with tears as she tried getting away, to press her face against my neck. I kissed her—softly at first, then deeper

"Maksim." She pulled her mouth away. "Don't distract me."

"Yes."

"Yes?"

"You asked me a question." I took her left hand and set the ring box in it. "The answer is yes."

Tianna tossed herself into my arms after a happy yelp. She hugged me, tightly, then proceeded to kiss my shoulder, my neck, my ear—every part of my face her mouth could read. I laughed softly.

"I still have to get you a ring." I told her.

"No rush." She leaned back to smile at me. "You said yes. You can't take it back."

"I can't?"

She smacked my shoulder. "Be serious for a second."

"You asked me to be your husband." I told her, softly. "I said yes. We've come a long way, soon to be Mrs. Demidov. There is no going back now. Besides, the construction guys are coming next week to start in on the new addition for your office. Once they break ground, you're stuck with me."

She giggled and hugged me again. "I love you, Maksim."

I sighed as she slid the silver band on my finger. "I love you too, Lover."

After I kissed her again, she pried herself from my arms. "I have to tell Echo."

I groaned.

The two of them were really close now. But I tapped her ass playfully and made my way into the bathroom.

As I showered, cleaned up my facial hair and brushed my teeth, I couldn't help marveling at how lucky I'd been.

"You will not mess this up, trickster boy." I told my reflection. "You've found a woman who doesn't want your money, who loves you and who puts up with your shit."

Shyly, I bowed my head, smiled then looked up again.

I walked out of the shower with a towel wrapped around my hips and entered the new closet we'd both had put in for ourselves. I dressed then pulled out a silver box I had in the corner behind my shoe rack. Inside, an old red box was tucked away beneath old photos of my parents and my grandfather. My heart raced as I entered the room again.

Tianna wasn't there but I found her in my office, working on my computer while furiously digging through the sketches she had littering my space.

"Would it help if you told me what you were looking for?" I asked.

Tianna looked up, air kissed at me then continued digging. "The design for the ivory wedding dress,"

She said. "My client wants some changes made and I figured I should do them while I'm fresh."

"You're panicking." I entered and took her hand to lead her around the desk. After she was sitting, I slipped to one knee and held the box out to her. "This belonged to my grandmother."

She opened it and gasped.

"I know it's not a diamond…"

"It's beautiful." She whispered. "Why did your mother not get this?"

"My mother wasn't the motherly type." I replied. "She handed me to my father and walked away before he could ask her to marry him."

"Babe—I'm sorry."

"No sadness today. Okay?"

She smiled at me then looked down at the ring again. Is that a ruby?"

"A red ruby set in white gold. If you don't like it—"

Her body crashing into mine stopped the words from tumbling out my lips. "It's beautiful and it would be my honour to wear it. You have to put it on me."

I pressed my lips into a thin line as I eased her back to the sofa and slipped the ring onto her finger. It slid on with no trouble at all, fitting perfectly. I kissed her, feeling my heart full to bursting.

Wrapping an arm around her, I set the box on the

floor out of the way. I then brought her down on top of me.

"Before you start something, Mr. Demidov." Tianna teased. "Echo and the Titans wants us to come by Thunder's place on the weekend for a little party."

"Knight said *little party*?" I asked.

She nodded.

"Oh boy. Knight doesn't know what the word *little* means."

She giggled. "We will cross that bridge later. In the meantime, I think you should show me a good time."

"I thought you had work to do."

"Do I have to hold you down and take it, Hermes?"

I smirked, my body hardening at the thought of her holding me down and having her way with me. Tianna laughed and sat up to remove her top and her bra. She took my palms and lifted them to her nipples. I pinched at them, loving the way she arched backward, shoving her warm breasts into my palms. I moaned as she rolled her hips down, pressing my clothed cock intimately against her.

By the time I rolled her over and trapped her body beneath mine, I could feel her happiness had soaked through the material of my track pants. I quickly removed the rest of her clothes and spread her wide to look at her.

"Maksim." She breathed.

I found her with a large finger, trailed it against the moist lips of her then plunged it in. Tianna spread her thighs wider for me, drove her hips up and sucked my finger deeper. I watched as her eyes rolled back and her lips parted.

"Do you like that, Tianna?" I demanded, pulling the finger out and driving two back in.

"Yes!" She cried. "More, please more."

"How about I do you one better?"

"Gimme."

Smiling, I pulled my hand back and climbed over her. This time as I plunged into her hot, wetness, Tianna surged upward, wrapped her arms around my neck and kissed me harder than she'd ever had. I growled, allowed her to suck on my tongue as her orgasm tore through her. She sank her nails into my back, sending pleasure rolling through me like ocean waves.

"*Ya lyublyu tebya.*" I whispered in Russian.

She opened her eyes. "It's the first time you've ever spoken to me in Russian." A smile traced her lips. "Can I guess what it means?"

I moaned. "Mmhmm."

"I love you too, Maksim."

I drove my hips in again, loving the way those words sounded tumbling from her lips. And just before my world shattered around me, I pulled her up and into my chest. I held onto the woman who'd made me kneel to her heart.

Yes, I loved Tianna Sharp, more than I could possibly explain to anyone.

I was in love and it felt as if I was flying.

The end

ABOUT ELLE JAMES

ELLE JAMES also writing as MYLA JACKSON is a *New York Times* and *USA Today* Bestselling author of books including cowboys, intrigues and paranormal adventures that keep her readers on the edges of their seats. With over eighty works in a variety of sub-genres and lengths she has published with Harlequin, Samhain, Ellora's Cave, Kensington, Cleis Press, and Avon. When she's not at her computer, she's traveling, snow skiing, boating, or riding her ATV, dreaming up new stories. Learn more about Elle James at www.ellejames.com

Website | Facebook | Twitter | GoodReads | Newsletter | BookBub | Amazon

Follow Elle!
www.ellejames.com
ellejames@ellejames.com

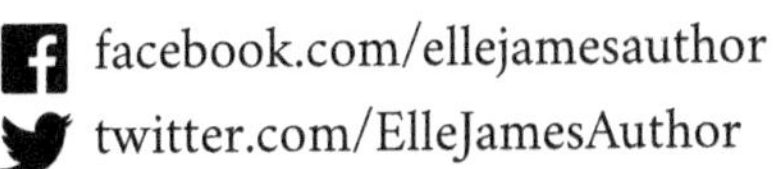
facebook.com/ellejamesauthor
twitter.com/ElleJamesAuthor

9 798710 104620